KISS
THE CANDY DAYS
HELLO

Kiss the Candy Days Hello is an amazing story that illustrates the struggles of an adolescent with diabetes and his ultimate triumph in overcoming his plight. The book beautifully depicts adolescent, child-parent and child-friendship conflict and the formula for resolution. This book is a must read for all parents and adolescents, not just those with diabetes. Vin Dacquino deserves a standing ovation for his outstanding work.

Dr. Richard A. Noto

Dr. Richard A. Noto is Chief of Pediatric Endocrinology, Diabetes and Endocrine Center for Children and Young Adults, Phelps Memorial Hospital, Sleepy Hollow, New York; Chief, Divison of Pediatric Endocrinology and Metabolism, Department of Pediatrics, Maria Fareri Children's Hospital at the Westchester Medical Center, Valhalla, New York; Chief of Pediatric Endocrinology and Metabolism, New York Medical College

****

Kiss the Candy Days Hello fills a gap in the literature for young adolescents and enables them to learn, understand, and relate to other teens having the same struggles with adolescence and diabetes. This is an invaluable resource for families, not only because of the diabetes education content that is expertly woven into a captivating storyline, but also for the psychological and social content that accurately captures the struggles that most adolescents encounter. A must read for teens with diabetes!

Dr. Alicia McAuliffe-Fogarty

Dr. Alicia McAuliffe-Fogarty established the Circle of Life Camp, Inc., a not-for-profit camp for children with diabetes in Albany, NY in 1996 at the age of eighteen. Currently, she is a Clinical Child Health Psychologist and serves on the Board of Directors of the Diabetes Education & Camping Association. She is the author of "Growing Up With Diabetes: What Children Want Their Parents to Know" and has published many articles. Dr. Alicia has received several awards for her efforts to improve the lives of children with diabetes.

Other Books by this Author:

Kiss the Candy Days Good-Bye
Sybil Ludington: The Call to Arms
Sybil Ludington: Discovering the Life of a Revolutionary War Hero
Hauntings of the Hudson River Valley
I.M Pei
Grandma Moses
Louis Pasteur
Max's Glasses

KISS
THE CANDY DAYS
HELLO

V.T. DACQUINO

A VTD EduCon Book

Published by
VTD EduCon Books
Mahopac, NY 10541

For further information go to:
www.vincentdacquino.com

ISBN: 1453651098
EAN-13: 9781453651094

Kiss the Candy Days Hello is a work of fiction and not
intended to portray any real person or events

TO

My mother for her years of love and dedication to her children and especially to me

AND TO

My wife, children, and grandchildren with all my love

Acknowledgments

The author gratefully expresses his appreciation to Alicia H. McAuliffe-Fogarty, Ph.D., Founder and Executive Director, Circle of Life Camp, Inc., John Clark, Jess Covey, Daniel Collins, Becky Plog and the Chin family for sharing their life experiences and knowledge of diabetes.

Special thanks to Dr. Richard Noto for generously sharing his time and knowledge, and to his office staff: Mary Alice Cucinel, Janis Kipp, and Jena Griffin.

Also a special thanks to Andrew LaGuardia, Director of Communications for the Maria Ferrari Children's Hospital at Westchester Medical Center; Terry Kroenert and the staff at the Children's Hospital.

Thanks to Janus Adams, Andy Campbell and to my friends and members of the Mahopac Library Writers Group for reading and commenting on drafts of the manuscript. And to Donald Wortzman for his generous help with publishing and Edward Ganbaum for his help with the cover. Extra special thanks to my son Vinny for lending his younger likeness to the front cover.

CHAPTER 1

My food was spread out party-like across the entire cafeteria table. I couldn't believe how hungry I was and checked to be sure nothing was missing. One over-stuffed turkey sandwich with extra mayo: check. Large bag potato chips: check. Granola bar: check. Three cherry juice drinks: check. One double-sized chunky chocolate chip cookie: check. My stomach growled and I wrapped my hands greedily around the turkey sandwich, but my mouth was too dry to eat anything. I put the sandwich down, opened one of the drinks, and guzzled it down in one gulp. The dryness was still there, so I followed the first one with the next two. My mouth felt a little better after the three drinks but my stomach was grumbling. I grabbed for the sandwich again lifting it to my mouth slowly.

"Don't bite that," a voice said.

I turned quickly and was face-to-face with Lou Ellen Parker.

1

Her long blonde hair was pushed behind her shoulders and her eyes were fixed on mine. I couldn't stop staring at her.

"Here," she said, smiling. She dropped a neatly folded piece of yellow paper next to my potato chips. I looked at it and glanced back at her confused. Was I supposed to put down my turkey sandwich and open her note in front of her? My stomach growled again and I think she heard it!

"You can read it later if you want, but you don't have to do what it says if you don't want to. It's just a suggestion," she said, and then, just like that, she walked away from me.

I was real thirsty again. I went over to the counter and bought three more drinks, relieved that there was no one in line. The cafeteria lady looked at me like I was up to something. I ignored her and returned to my table and my food. I took a huge bite out of the wedge and stared down at the note in front of me as I chewed. Suddenly, I started thinking about where I was. Was this thing with Lou Ellen some kind of joke? I checked out all of the eighth grade tables to see if anyone looked suspicious. A couple of kids were looking in my direction but no one looked very guilty. I took another huge bite of the sandwich and examined the bunch of kids gathered at the door she had gone through.

After a lot of chewing, swallowing and drinking, I picked up Lou Ellen's note. It was really weird. The side facing up was blank but the other side had "To Mary Jane" written on it.

"Huh?" I said. "To Mary Jane?"

I opened it quickly; it was signed "Your best friend, Lou Ellen."

Dear Mary Jane,

I can't stand it anymore. He's so hot! His eyes make me melt. I love the way his brown hair brushes to the side. I have tried everything to get him to notice me but he acts like I'm invisible. I can't take it anymore. I have a plan that I have to try at lunch today. I am going to---

Suddenly, there was a commotion coming from the door of the cafeteria and I looked up to see Lou Ellen charging at me! I knew I had to be dreaming all of this. Before I could say anything she grabbed the note out of my hand, dropped another one in front of me, and went running out of the cafeteria. I just sat there watching her leave, and then picked up the new note. This one had "To JJ" written on one side:

Dear JJ,

I know you don't really know me very well, but I am going to be having a birthday party next month. It's only going to be for a few kids so I don't want to talk about it at school. I can add you to my invitation list if you would like to come. Call me if you want. My number is 242-7707.

Lou Ellen Parker

I'm not a genius, but I figured out pretty quickly what had happened: Lou Ellen had given me the wrong note the first time! The one that said I was "hot!" I laughed so hard I almost choked myself to death. But what happened after that wasn't so funny. I had to go to the bathroom real badly and I wasn't sure I could make it. I stuffed Lou Ellen's note into my pocket then hurried out as fast as I could; I made it to a toilet bowl just in time.

I washed my face and hands and looked at myself in the mirror. I looked pretty awful and felt even worse. When I went back to my table my social studies teacher, Mr. Papalardi, was standing over it. "Is this all your food, J.J.? Are you okay?" he asked.

"I'm fine," I said. "I just had to go to the bathroom real fast."

He smiled and counted my juice cartons, "You're probably going to have to go again when you finish here. Are you sure you're okay? You look pretty pale."

"I just have a little virus or something," I said.

He squinted with one eye and said, "Are you sure this isn't just a plan to get out of tomorrow's test?"

"No, honest," I said, "I---"

He laughed. "I'm teasing you. But you might want to check with the nurse if you don't feel better."

"I'm fine," I said. But I wasn't fine. Something weird was going on with me. It had been going on for almost a whole month, and I wasn't about to tell my problem to Mr. Papalardi ...or my parents.

****

I struggled to climb each stair one at a time with the flashlight off. From the kitchen I could hear the soft whir of the refrigerator motor and made my way toward it. Light flooded the room as I opened the door and grabbed the orange juice. I guzzled almost the whole quart, put the container back, and

5

moved out of the kitchen. I could hear the ticking of the clock over the fireplace in the living room as I passed through it. My eyes adjusted to the darkness again and the two doors at the end of the hallway appeared slowly. I slipped barefooted toward my father's office as quietly as possible, but stopped still at my parents' bedroom to listen for the sleeping pig noises. He was snoring loudly, as usual. I listened harder for sounds from my mother; she was sleeping quietly, but she was a heavy sleeper and I was less afraid of waking her.

The door to the office was unlocked and the bottom swished softly against the carpet as I pushed into the small room. The little green numbers glared up at me from the clock radio on his desk: "3 AM." I switched on the flashlight and pointed it to the bookshelf. *KISS THE CANDY DAYS GOOD-BYE* was where it had always been. I grabbed for it and tucked it quickly into my pajama bottoms as I worked my way past their door and back downstairs to my bedroom. The small lamp at the side of my bed was on and I snuggled close to it to begin reading the book my father had written, but I couldn't get myself to open it. I sat there with the book on my lap and read the back cover out loud:

"Something strange is happening to Jimmy James. He can't seem to satisfy his hunger or

6

thirst, goes to the bathroom too frequently, and always feels irritable and dizzy. Jimmy tries to ignore these awful feelings and concentrate on gaining weight for his junior-high school wrestling team.

But to his surprise he keeps losing weight and continues to feel strange, until the day he collapses and is rushed to the hospital---"

My head started spinning. I got up and dragged myself to the bathroom. The scale was out where I had left it and I got on. Two more pounds were gone. I turned toward the toilet and peed for a real long time and then drank from the faucet avoiding my face in the mirror. The water felt good in my mouth---but not in my stomach. I was pretty sure I knew what was happening … my father had put a curse on me by writing a book on diabetes.

CHAPTER 2

There had to be a connection. Ten years before I was born my father wrote a best selling book about a kid with diabetes. The weirdest part was that my father never had diabetes. The whole book was based on research. It was no surprise that when I came along my parents were so thrilled with how great the book was doing they named me Jimmy James Johnson, also known as "J.J." So why would it be such a surprise that I'd end up with diabetes like the real Jimmy James? I pulled the covers over my head and tried to drown out my mother's voice.

"J.J., get up. You'll be late for school," my mother shouted.

I was way too weak to shout up to her and squeezed my pillow over my head to drown her out.

"J.J., did you hear your mother?"

I knew what was coming next and counted to three before he was downstairs with me. "Don't

8

you have your big social studies test today? I don't
want to hear any excuses for staying home. You
have five minutes to get up. Breakfast is on the
table. Mr. Papalardi warned that you needed a good
score on this test today. Get a move on." He turned
away and walked back up the stairs before I could
answer, and it was just as well. My mouth was too
dry to say anything and my bladder felt like it was
going to burst. I dragged myself to the bathroom
for a drink of water and then peed even longer than
the night before.

After struggling to get dressed and get through
my doorway, I saw him at the top of the stairs.

"I'm up," I said. My voice didn't even sound
like mine.

"Were you up late reading last night?" he asked.
"I told you to pace yourself when you study.
Cramming the night before doesn't do much good.
You look terrible. Jump in the shower when you're
done eating. It'll help you to feel refreshed."

"I'll be all right," I told him.

"Eat and take a shower," he said. "I'll drive you
in. I don't have anything pressing and can spare the
time today."

****

As the car drove along, I kept my face toward
the window thinking about how I had looked in the

mirror before we left. There were dark circles under my eyes like the ones my mother gets when she's tired.

"Are you ready for the big test?" my father asked.

I almost turned to face him and stopped myself. "I'm ready," I said.

He didn't push it. He just kept driving until we reached the school and pulled to the curb. "Good luck with it," he said, then grabbed my hand. "J, is there something you aren't telling me? Your mother and I are concerned with you lately. You don't seem like yourself. Is there something you'd like to talk about?"

It was my chance to come out with it. I could have just blurted the whole thing out to him right then and there---but I couldn't.

"I'm fine," I lied. "I've just been worrying about school and stuff."

"We're here to help you if you need it," he said. "Why don't you ask one of your friends from school to come over and study with you? You never have any friends over. If you want we can even get a tutor. Eighth grade is---"

"I'm fine," I said again. "I really have to get into school."

He gave a big sigh, handed me my lunch, and said, "Maybe we can talk tonight after supper. I think it might also be a good idea to make an appointment with Dr. Ellis. It's been a while since your last check up. Good luck on that test."

I worked my way to the second floor and almost couldn't make it to the landing. I put all of my things into my locker, except my books for social studies. I was wishing that my test wasn't first period, but wishing doesn't always make things happen, especially when you wish for things to go right.

Mr. Papalardi was looking at me a little weird and I was happy when he stopped staring and stepped outside with one of the other teachers. When he came back in he passed out copies of the test, gave us directions and told us we could get started. The test seemed okay, but by the time I was done with it, *I* wasn't. A sick feeling was starting in my stomach.

That's when something hit my leg. I looked down and saw a familiar piece of folded yellow paper at my foot. I glanced up at Mr. Papalardi who was talking to someone on the classroom phone then picked up the yellow note. It said *"For J.J.'s Eyes ONLY."* I looked back at Lou Ellen and she was smiling a real sweet kind of smile. I turned away from her and opened the note to read it; when I looked up, Mr. Papalardi was standing over me frowning at the note in my hand.

He took my test paper and said, "Come with me."

11

I was going to say I wasn't cheating, but I felt real sick.

Before I could help myself I was vomiting all over his shoes. I wanted to try to say something, but all I could think of was the vomit all over the floor and the little yellow note in the middle of it. He led me to the door and I went with him trying to avoid looking at the other kids. My mouth tasted like puke and I could see spots of it on my clothes.

"How are you feeling?" he asked when we were in the hall.

"Embarrassed," I said. "But not as sick. I'm sorry about your shoes. I wasn't cheating. I---"

"I know you enough to know you wouldn't cheat, J.J. Let's concentrate on how you are doing. Can you walk?" he asked.

"Yeah," I said.

He turned to the hall monitor who was standing there and said, "Get him down to the nurse. Use the elevator." He looked back at me and said, "Don't worry about anything except feeling better. We'll worry about taking the test later. Everything will be fine here."

When we got into the nurse's office, the nurse was waiting for me. There were no other kids in there and I was real glad. I didn't feel like talking to any kids this morning.

"What's up, J.J? Tell me what's been going on," the nurse said.

"I really have to go the bathroom first," I told her.

"Have you been feeling sick?"

"Uh, huh," I said, and hurried into the bathroom in her office. After I washed my face and hands, I looked at myself in the mirror and felt like crying. The circles under my eyes were darker than ever and I had stains on my shirt. I also wished I had mouth wash or tooth paste to clean the bad taste out of my mouth.

When I pulled open the door the nurse was standing there smiling at me. "Why don't you come and sit in here for a little while? I called your parents and they are going to come to pick you up."

"Is it okay if I have something to drink?" I asked.

She gave me a small can of ginger ale and put me on a cot with the curtains closed around me; I hated being alone in there. All I kept thinking about was throwing up on Mr. Papalardi's shoes in front of the whole class and Lou Ellen's note in the middle of the mess. I was sure that Lou Ellen wasn't thinking that I was so "hot" now!

After about ten minutes I heard my father's voice, "How is he doing?"

"He's resting," the nurse said.

"I put in a call to the pediatrician. We're headed straight over to him," my father told her.

I pulled open the curtain and my mother sort of smiled at me and asked if I was okay. She had a plastic bag with clean clothes in it for me.

"I haven't been feeling well and threw up in class," I said.

She had the dark circles below her eyes like mine and her face was saying that I should have told her about this at breakfast. Why didn't I trust her and say something? But she didn't talk. She handed me the bag and I changed my shirt behind the curtain.

The nurse said, "You'll have to sign him out. Would you like to use the wheel chair? We---"

"No," I said. "I want to walk."

My father nodded to her that it would be okay and he lightly touched one arm while my mother took the other. I knew how it would look to any kids who were watching, but I really didn't feel strong enough to walk on my own.

There were almost no kids in the hall when we left the nurse and headed for the front door, but the principal stopped us as we passed his office. He's a real nice guy and we like each other.

"Are you okay?"

I tried to smile. "We're going to check it out now," I said, "but I already know what's wrong."

My father looked at me surprised, and I looked right at him when I said, "I think I have diabetes."

V.T. Dacquino

CHAPTER 3

My father kept asking me questions about how I was feeling as we drove along and something suddenly starting rumbling inside of me. I could feel my temper rising. It was like I had swallowed a gorilla that was taking control of me. And the gorilla didn't want to hear him anymore.

"Shut up," I shouted at him. "Stop asking me questions. I don't want to talk about it! You are the one who did this to me. Why did you have to write that stupid book? Why?"

He started to say something but my mother stopped him. She saw me crying.

We didn't say much to each other on the way to the doctor's office and I felt exhausted and real weird, like something bad was about to happen and I didn't know what. Was I going to throw up again? Was I going to faint? I knew for sure that I *was* going to wet my pants if they didn't get me inside soon.

16

My father dropped me and my mother at the door of the office building and I found a bathroom in the lobby. When I was finished going I drank from the faucet to get rid of my cotton-mouth taste. My mother was standing there looking toward the doors, waiting for my father who came running in. I felt real sorry for both of them because they looked even worse than I felt. My father looked like maybe he had been crying and I wished I could take back what I had said to him. He stared at me and I let him put his arms around me. I wanted to say I was sorry and that he should quit squeezing me because I couldn't breathe, but I let him keep hugging me and just cried with him. When he was done we both went into the men's room to wash our faces.

Dr. Ellis has been my pediatrician since I was born and nobody knows me better. I felt real scared about going into his office because he never lies. I knew this was the time for answers and I tried to smile when we walked in; he was standing there waiting for us. His hair was red and spiked up. My father said it's because he's around kids all day and likes looking cool. Today he just looked worried.

"What's up, champ?" he said.

"I haven't been feeling well," I answered.

He put his hand on my chin and looked into my face, "I can see that."

He told me to take my shoes off and go to the scale with the nurse. When he saw my weight he frowned and looked at the clipboard on the table. "Has he been eating?" he asked my parents. "He's down ten pounds from the last visit."

My parents looked shocked.

"I've been eating more, not less," I said, "and I've been real thirsty? I had six juice drinks for lunch."

"Have you been going to the bathroom a lot?" He asked.

"Yes," I said. "My mouth is dry right now and I just went to the bathroom again downstairs."

"Get yourself a tall glass of water from the water bottle," he said, then he turned to the nurse and told her to give me a plastic cup. He told me to go into the bathroom and try to pee in the cup and leave it on the back of the toilet.

I did what he said and had no trouble filling the cup.

He was talking quietly to my parents when I came out. The nurse went into the bathroom right behind me. When he finished talking to my parents the nurse came up to him with the cup and whispered something to him.

"Let's get a finger stick," he told her, "We'll check his blood sugar."

While she was out getting what he wanted he asked my parents to sit down. The nurse came back to me and said, "This will hurt a little but it's nothing you can't handle." She pricked my finger with a little trigger thing and it made me jump; a tiny spot of blood appeared. She dabbed the blood onto the thing she was holding. After a couple seconds, Doctor Ellis looked at it and said. "J.J., do you remember the book your father wrote about Jimmy James?"

"Yes," I answered, and looked over at my father. He looked like he was going to cry.

"I'm afraid you may have inherited more than Jimmy James' initials. Do you remember what diabetes is?"

I knew he was going to say it. I knew before we ever got to his office, but it was different actually hearing the word come from him. I felt like throwing up again, or crying, because I couldn't remember anything about diabetes except what my father said to me about it once, "It's something you can be thankful you don't have."

Dr. Ellis started explaining it, but it was like his words weren't going into my ears. His mouth was moving and I wasn't hearing anything he was saying. It was like the word *diabetes* was echoing in my head louder and louder.

"You know that having diabetes means that your body's ability to produce insulin has been impaired," he said. "Insulin is a hormone produced by Beta cells in the pancreas that allows cells to process glucose into energy."

He stopped and looked into my face for a second then took a piece of paper and started drawing something, but I was watching his lips move as he talked and trying to see what my parents were thinking. My father was shaking his head a lot like he knew exactly what Doctor Ellis was talking about.

"The food you eat with carbohydrate in it, that's everything besides protein and fat, is broken down into sugar that your body uses for energy. Insulin unlocks the doors to all of the cells in your body to let the sugar in so that you have energy to walk, run, and go to school. When your body isn't making enough insulin, it starts to break down your own body fat as an energy source because your cells need energy from someplace. That's why you were losing weight and feeling weak and tired. The only choice we have is to give the body the insulin it's missing through injections. That means you're going to have to take over for what your body used to do automatically."

I knew he was saying things that were important, but the only thing going into my ears was, "blah, blah, blah, blah" and "take over for your body."

"Suppose I don't want to take over for my body?" I heard myself ask. "Suppose I just want to

20

be the way I've always been?" I felt myself getting angry and my eyes were getting hot.

"J.J., I wish I had better news for you. I've known you your whole life and I can't think of any of my patients I'm more proud of --- even if you did try to bite me a few times when you were younger." He smiled his kind of smile and tapped me on the side of my chin. "Diabetes is something that is going to change your life; there are no two ways about that. We all have to deal with change. It's part of life. Things will be a little different for you now. No one's denying that. But this isn't a choice we're giving you here. Fate has made a choice for you, and you'll have to learn to live with that choice."

I didn't answer.

"I'm going to put you in the hospital for a couple of days to get you feeling better. We have specialists there who will talk to you about what all of this means and help you get back to school."

I was going to ask him how I was supposed to get back to normal with diabetes, but I just kept quiet.

He looked at all three of us one at a time. I've known all of you since J.J. was born, and if there is anything I know most about you, it's that you are a team. That has never been more important than it is now. I'm going to call the hospital to make arrangements and I need you to head over there."

21

CHAPTER 4

Spring was definitely happening and I looked out at all the trees starting to bud as we drove along the parkway. I tried to keep my mind on the lawns and flowers so I wouldn't have to think of what was really happening. I knew what hospital Dr. Ellis was talking about. I had been there lots of times. The children's wing is part of the county hospital; only, the children's part has its own entrance with a huge statue of a teddy bear sitting in front of it. The hedges are cut into shapes of animals and the sign over the door says: "Family Entrance." The trash pails have lady bugs painted on them and they make my mother want to cry because her father loved lady bugs. The glass doors open when people step up to them and nothing looks anything like a hospital after you enter. The lobby has a huge aquarium with amazing schools of blue and yellow fish. Behind that is a large open space with a piano so the hospital can run programs for patients who are well enough to come down to see them. On the left is a gift shop where parents can buy anything their kid could wish for---except not being sick.

We pulled into the parking lot and I expected my father to lead me to those doors, but he didn't.

"Dr. Ellis instructed us to go in another way," he said. "We have to get you checked in."

I looked in the direction my father was pointing. A helicopter was parked in front of the doors! The sign over them read, "Children's Entrance-Emergency Room."

"That's the helicopter they use to bring in emergency victims," he said. "Not every patient is lucky enough to walk through these doors."

He smiled and walked next to me, but I didn't feel lucky, just scared.

There weren't any fish tanks or pianos when we walked in, just a soda machine and some sofas and chairs. A lady was behind a desk and she smiled at us. My mother went up to her and talked to her for a few minutes while my father stood with me and put his hand on my shoulder. I felt sick and wanted to go home. I felt like I was going to throw up again; I needed to drink and go to the bathroom.

"J.J.?" my mother said, loudly, "they need to ask us some questions but they'd like you to go inside. One of us can go with you and one of us can stay here."

"I want *you* to come with me," I said to my mother. I looked at my father and he gave me a sort of sad smile. "It's fine," he said. We went inside and I went into the bathroom. When I got out they put me in a small room in a place called *triage*, which was a place for patients who needed help in a hurry. A real pretty nurse with green eyes like a cat's came in and she started to do all the normal stuff they usually do in Dr. Ellis's office. But then she wheeled in this stupid pole with a plastic bag on it. The nurse was telling me everything about what was going on, only I still didn't feel like listening to her talk about diabetes. She stuck a needle in my arm attached to a tube and it hurt even though she said it wouldn't. She said that the stuff in the bag was insulin and fluid to rehydrate me. Three hours later, when they were finally done doing more things to me, she said I could go up to the third floor. My mother gathered my things and my father came in the room with a paper in his hand.

"I have a list of things that you'll need while you're here," he said. "I'll get your pajamas and a couple of your sweat suits and a pair of your jeans from home."

When I figured out what he was saying, I said, "I can wear regular clothes?"

"Yeah," he said. "You'll be doing a lot of things here. You aren't going to be in bed the whole time.

24

They'll explain everything to you when you get upstairs. I won't be gone long."

He reached out and hugged me again and it felt real weird because it's not like he always hugged me before today. It made me choke up because I knew he was feeling pretty lousy about everything I said and because of what was happening to me. I turned quickly to see if the nurse had been watching us hug, but her back was turned to us.

"We'd better get upstairs," my mother said. "The nurse is waiting."

I waved good-bye to my father and the nurse put me on a bed with wheels and took us to the elevator that went up to the third floor. She was asking questions and talking about little things but the movement of the elevator was making me sick. "Please, God," I said to myself, "don't let me throw up in front of her."

I was relieved when the elevator stopped and the doors opened. She rolled me past a large desk where a nurse told us what room we were going to. I was glad we were going into a room because I hated being on a bed in the hall with everybody looking at me. It felt like I hadn't slept in about a week and I was more thirsty than usual. When we got to the room I was sort of surprised. The room wasn't anything like I had expected. There were no other patients in it and it had a private bathroom.

V.T. Dacquino

The nurse helped me off the bed and into the bathroom.

"We have a couple things we'll need to do right away," the nurse said when I came out. "Are you feeling okay?"

"No," I said. "I think I have to throw up."

I went back into the bathroom and bent over the bowl. I couldn't believe how much came out of me. I didn't even care that the nurse was standing there. I felt better when I was done and my mother wiped my forehead with a cloth. After the nurse did all of the things she was supposed to do, the doctor from the hospital came in. He was short and dark with glasses and he had an Indian accent.

He looked down at his clipboard and then at me. "You must be J.J."

The nurse, my mother, and I all said yes at exactly the same time and as sick as I was, I had to laugh with them.

"I have been expecting you," he said. "I am Doctor Raymond. Officially, I am a pediatric endocrinologist on staff at the hospital here, but more importantly I will be your physician while you are here. I just spoke with Dr. Ellis, your pediatrician. He asked me to speak with you and get you feeling better. He will try to visit with you later tonight."

"I just threw up," I told him.

"Yes," he said. "I think we are going to skip dinner. I see the nurse has set up your I.V. for you. We are going to try to get you hydrated again. You should drink as much water or diet ginger ale as you would like. The insulin will help you to feel much better. I wish I could tell you that it will make you feel better right now, but the truth is it will take a while. You should feel much better by evening."

While he was talking, a nurse came in wearing a Mickey Mouse pajama-like pant-suit and the doctor stepped back right onto her foot. She made a kind of squealing sound and everyone in the room jumped. Dr. Raymond laughed a weird kind of laugh and apologized to her over and over again until she left to talk to my mother in the hall. It was pretty funny considering the mood I was in.

"Well, you will have nothing to worry about," he said finally. "We have a nurse educator here who will work with you and teach you everything you will need to know. She will probably be in to see you any time now. There are going to be many people running in and out of here for a while. I want you to rest as best you can, but these people are necessary. You look shaky. Are you still feeling sick to your stomach?"

"Yes," I said.

"You should not be surprised if you get sick a couple of more times today. It is all quite normal

27

right now." He patted my hand and walked out into the hall with my mother.

Two minutes after he walked out, my father poked his head in to say he was back with my things. The nurse with the Mickey Mouse uniform also came back in again and introduced herself as Mary Montgomery. My father handed her the bag with my pajamas and she asked me to put on the bottoms. She said she would help me with the top because of the IV, and then pulled the curtain around my bed.

My father stayed in the hall with my mother while I got dressed under the covers. I didn't feel like taking chances with nurses poking their heads in.

"You can call me Mary," the nurse said when she came back in. She opened the curtain and wrote her name on a white board that was hanging on my wall before checking the pole and plastic bag. I hated that bag and I know the nurse knew it because she looked at me and smiled a sad smile.

"I grabbed your books in case you feel like studying later," my father said from behind her. The nurse finished up what she was doing and my father stepped closer to the bed. "For now you should just relax. The good news is that you're in good hands now. The people here really know what they're doing." He started to say something else, but a woman came in behind him. The place was like a circus.

The woman behind my father wasn't wearing any uniform. She wore glasses and a lab coat over a pant suit. She introduced herself as Margaret Boyd and said I could call her Meg. She looked a lot like Sarah Palin, the Governor of Alaska who ran for Vice President. She smiled at me and said. "J.J., I'm the diabetes educator here at the hospital and my job is to help you learn more about your diabetes. By now you know that the initial tests your pediatrician has done all indicate that you have diabetes. I know you know a little about it because of your father's book." She glanced at my father, smiled, and said, "It was one of the first books I read about diabetes when *I* was in eighth grade. It's a real good book, and I still recommend it to my young patients. Jimmy and Margaret are wonderful examples of how kids overcome challenges and carry on with their lives."

She was carrying a pile of things and set them on the bed. "A few things have changed with diabetes treatment since Jimmy was diagnosed, and we want to be sure you are all aware of the most up-to-date information. We've already started you on some insulin to help you feel better, J.J. You probably feel like you have cotton-mouth and are very tired. In a couple of days here, you---"

"Why a couple of days?" I said.

"Didn't Dr. Raymond or Dr. Ellis mention that we'll need to keep you a few days to help you to get your energy back? You won't be here long. Our goal is to get you back to school as soon as possible. If you can bear with me I'd really like to start with the basics. Besides regular injections you are going to have to learn to balance what you eat and are going to have to test your blood sugar regularly."

She took out a small box from her things and opened it, and then she picked out the same kind of PDA-looking instrument Dr. Ellis had used to test my blood in his office. "I'm sure Dr. Ellis used one of these on you earlier. It's called a glucometer. We just call it a meter. It's used to check your blood sugar." She picked up a little vial and said, "These are test strips. You may have seen your doctor insert one of these into the meter. Once it's inserted the meter beeps and goes on." She pointed to a number on the screen and made sure all three of us could see what she was doing. "This screen displays a code. The code needs to match the numbers on the vile that I took the test strip from. They *must* match. She pointed to the numbers and said, "See here how they match? Once you see that they do, you're ready to test your blood."

She took my index finger and touched the pen-like thing against the side of the tip. After she pressed the trigger a spot of my blood appeared the way it did in the office. "It's better if you don't use the very tip of the finger," she said. "The tip is more sensitive and you touch things more with that part of your finger. Go off to the side a little the way I did. You should also rotate what fingers you use. Don't use the same finger over and over again," she said.

She raised my finger and touched the tip of the test strip to the blood. The machine beeped and started counting down. In about 10 seconds the word 'HI' showed up. "Ordinarily, a number will appear where the word 'HI' appears," she said. "Since your body hasn't had enough time to process the insulin yet, your blood sugar is out of range for the meter. The goal is to have you somewhere between 80 and 120. She discarded the used strip and the meter turned off by itself. "After it turns off," she said, "you should put the meter back in the box, put the cap back on the lancet and discard it with the used test strip, and then record it in this." She took a little book out of the box. "This is your self-test log book. You need to record the date, time, and results every time you test."

"You'll need to check your blood sugar before every meal and before you go to bed. While you're here the nurses will also check it through the night. This is going to be an important part of your daily routine which is why I needed to go through this carefully for you. This kit is for you and you need to start using it as soon as possible."

She paused to see if we were all listening. I made a face and my mother gave me an "I-wish-it were-me" smile.

"Your readings are affected by what you eat," Meg continued. She smiled and looked at all three of us. "I know it seems like a lot to learn but it will all become very natural. We'll spend a lot of time tomorrow going through the ins and outs of food and nutrition."

She paused again and looked at me. "Are you feeling sick?"

"Yes," I said. "I already threw up when I got here and I have to go to the bathroom pretty bad."

"A lot of that will change as we get more insulin into you," she said, and then she stepped back and helped me move the pole with my insulin into the bathroom so I could pee. When I came out she was still there and my parents were in the hall talking to each other. She talked to me about a lot of things and even talked about what else my parents were going to have to know. She said I shouldn't rely on them to do everything and it was better if I knew what had to be done for myself. I was glad when she finally said she was leaving and I could rest awhile.

I put my head back against my pillow and Doctor Ellis walked in with my parents!

"Getting some rest?" he asked.

"No," I said.

He smiled and said, "Hey, quit complaining. Look at all the fun you're having."

"Yeah, right," I said.

He looked at my I.V and checked a clip board he was holding. "You know you're all going to have a real busy day tomorrow. I stopped by to give you a heads-up on the schedule. The good news J, is that there will be room in your schedule for all of the activities we provide. Don't expect to spend much time in bed. You're going to be kept very busy for pretty much all of your three or four days with us."

"I thought you said only *two* days?" I asked.

"We'll have to play it all as it goes," he said. "Your blood sugar is pretty high. You need to feel comfortable and get some diabetes education, like knowing how to give yourself injections, learning what causes low and high blood sugar and learning what you have to do for those conditions, and concentrating on nutrition. Nutrition is something you are going to have to pay real close attention to. I'm not saying you have to learn everything you need to know about your diabetes in this visit, but there are some basics you'll have to learn before you leave. A lot depends on how quickly you learn and how willing you are to learn. I won't lie to you, J., there's a lot to learn, but you'll have time to do

33

other things. Did you know that we have a computer room, an art room and a library? Trust me. The time is going to go by fast and there's no chance of getting bored. Get some rest for tonight and try not to worry about anything. Your mother is staying with you through the night and you can watch television if you like. Things slow down after 8 pm but there will be a lot of people coming in and out pretty much through the night."

He reached out and I shook his hand.

"You'll do fine," he said. "I have faith in you."

CHAPTER 5

I guess I was pretty exhausted because I slept until 8:15. My father left at 8 o'clock to get things done at home. Meg told him he would be needed at the hospital tomorrow with my mother to learn about my diabetes. I put my television on real low at about 8:30, but I didn't feel like watching it. By 9:00 my mother was asleep in the chair in the corner tucked under a blanket with a pillow behind her head and her feet propped up on a stool. She looked real comfortable and I was happy for her because I knew she was pretty worn out from everything that had happened. The IV was still dripping away into my arm. I just didn't know what to do with myself. It was awful quiet and I was bored with no one to talk to. The last nurse in asked me if she should turn off the television and I said yes. No one came for a while after that. I hated being in there. I almost pressed the emergency call-

35

button the nurse had shown me so someone would come in, but I didn't have to.

"I see you're awake," my mother said. Her voice made me jump.

"Yeah," I told her. "I've been awake a pretty long time."

"Why didn't you wake me?" she asked.

"You needed to sleep," I said.

She smiled and came over to my bedside. "Always looking after me."

I felt proud to hear her say that, because it was true. If anything happened to my mother I don't know what I would do. I started remembering how I had felt last year when one of the kids in my class lost his mother to cancer. I kept thinking that something was going to happen to my mother or father.

"You could have put your television on," she said.

"I hate television," I said. She squeezed my hand real tight.

"You gave us a scare today. How long were you feeling sick? Why didn't you tell one of us what was going on?"

She looked like she was about to cry and I couldn't look at her. "You know how much we worry about you. We---"

"That's why I didn't tell you," I interrupted. "I didn't want you to worry, in case it wasn't anything

36

serious. I thought maybe all those things would just go away. It was only a few weeks."

She didn't say anything for a long time, and then she said," Are you feeling better?"

"Yes," I said.

She waited a long time again before saying, "I know this all seems frightening to you right now, but Daddy and I will help you to see this all through. Daddy knows a lot about this because of his book---"

"He wrote his book a long time ago," I said. "And Meg said things have changed a lot with diabetes since then. And no two cases are the same."

"That's true," she said, but your father and I are going to learn everything we'll need to know to help you."

"Meg said I have to learn to be independent."

She frowned and looked like she was trying not to get angry. "Meg had a lot to say didn't she?"

"Yes," I said.

She took my hand. "I'm proud of you for handling all of this so well today."

I looked at her trying to sound brave, but I couldn't think of anything brave to say to her. "What if I mess up the injections and eat the wrong stuff?"

"I know this is all very frightening and serious, J.J., but there are millions of children out there with diabetes, and some of them are a lot younger than you. If all of them can make it, so can you. Nobody likes being different but everyone is different in some way. It's how we handle who we are that makes all the difference in the world. Do you remember Dr. Ellis and the nurse saying that?"

"Are *you* different?" I asked.

She thought about it for a second, and then said, "I'm a lot shyer than most people. I'm happiest when I'm with you and Daddy and don't like being around other people very much. When I was in school, I used to stay to myself most of the time. I guess you are a lot like me in that way. Daddy is different because he loves to be in front of people talking about his books or signing autographs or conducting workshops."

"Did you know Daddy a long time before you married him?"

"I did," she said. "We knew each other since high school when my parents moved us here from upstate." She smiled and looked at me. "You've heard that story a dozen times."

"I know," I said, and then I just heard the words coming out of me. "A girl in my class thinks I'm hot."

She sat up real straight and said, "She thinks you're *what*?"

"Hot," I said. I felt myself smiling and getting red and we just burst out laughing real hard. When we stopped laughing I told her all about Lou Ellen's note and we started our laughing fit again. I loved hearing her laugh like that.

"So," she said, "Is Lou Ellen *hot*?"

I laughed and said yes, but I felt real tired and sick. She was trying to think of something else to say. I held my stomach because I felt like throwing up again. "I can't talk anymore right now," I said. "My stomach hurts again."

She looked real scared and I wished I hadn't said anything about my stomach. I wanted to go back to laughing with her. But I felt too sick and tired.

CHAPTER 6

The hospital is different in the daytime and there isn't time to be bored or to worry. The good thing was that I felt a little better and they gave me real food. All three of us had things to learn and do after breakfast. The computer room was cool and the woman in there said I could send and get email if I wanted. I checked my school email to see if anyone had written to me. There was one email from Mr. Papalardi and seven from Lou Ellen. The one from Mr. Papalardi was about feeling better and not worrying about the kids or homework, but the ones from Lou Ellen were weird. They were about her friends and things she liked to do and the plans she was making for her birthday. The last one was the one that really got me nervous---she asked if she and Mary Jane could come to the hospital to visit with me tonight. I remembered that Meg said it would be fine to have visitors during visiting hours if I liked.

I sat with my fingers above the keyboard for a long time before I finally typed, "yes."

By the time visiting hours came I was pretty exhausted; I learned more in a day there than I learned in a week at school, and besides, I was thinking about Lou Ellen coming to see me. I ate dinner and spent a lot of time trying to figure out what to wear. I combed my hair a couple of different ways, and changed my clothes a couple of times, but ended up with my hair the regular way and my favorite jeans and shirt. The nurse said we could meet in the computer room if I didn't want to meet in my own room. My parents were dying to meet her and I said they could, but only if they promised to leave right after that.

She got there around six-thirty and she looked amazing. Her blonde hair was straight and she had a little make-up on. Mary Jane looked pretty good too. I looked at my father and he had his eyebrows raised. My mother was smiling with her seal-of-approval look and I knew she was thinking about Lou Ellen saying I was "hot."

"Hi," Lou Ellen said. Mary Jane said hi too, but my parents just stood there. I coughed to give them the hint to say something and *leave*; they looked embarrassed when they finally got the hint.

"It's nice to meet the two of you," my mother said. My father stuck out his hand and they shook it one at a time. I let my expression say, "Okay, *go now*."

When we were alone, Lou Ellen asked, "Is this the computer you answered me on?"

"Yeah," I said.

"You don't have to be in bed?" she asked.

"No," I said.

"You look pretty good," she added.

I guess I looked up at her too fast, because she looked embarrassed.

"I mean, you don't look sick. Don't you have to wear pajamas and stay in bed and stuff?"

"No," I said.

She looked around the room and was quiet for a few minutes, and then she said, "Oh, I almost forgot. This is for you. I didn't bring you candy, because---well, you know."

I must have looked shocked. Did Mr. Papalardi tell on me? Did the whole class know what was wrong? I felt sick inside. I was remembering what happened in class and throwing up and stuff and I was thinking about what the kids were going to say when I got back to school. I didn't want them feeling sorry for me or treating me like something was wrong with me. And I didn't want them making fun of me or saying stupid things.

"Are you okay?" she asked.

"I'm fine," I said.

She looked down at the present in my hand, "You can open it now if you want. It's from both of us." Mary Jane looked at me and smiled. I opened the present slowly and there was a box with a million pieces of tape on it. I finally got it open and looked inside. Something was wrapped in about ten sheets of tissue paper.

It was heavy and silver: A picture frame, with an autographed picture of Lou Ellen and Mary Jane in their cheerleading uniforms, smiling.

"Do you like it?" she asked. "We wanted to get you something special but couldn't think of anything good to get you."

"I really like it," I said.

The three of us stood there not saying anything for a while until Lou Ellen said, "All of my plans are pretty set for my birthday party. You're going to come, right? It's June 7, a Friday. We were going to have it at the skating rink but everyone does that and then we were thinking about having it at the Pizza Palace but that's not very private and we don't want a hundred kids crashing the party. You know what I mean?"

I didn't answer. I looked down at their pictures. Their names were written in black Scripto pen. It was kind of like an autographed rock star's photo, like Brittany Spears or Hannah Montana. And it said "Get well" on it.

"When are you getting out of here?" Lou Ellen asked.

"In about two more days," I said.

"Can you come back to school right after that?" she asked.

"I think so," I said.

"That's cool," she answered.

We stood there quiet again and then I couldn't believe what she said. "You shouldn't worry about what the kids think about your throwing up in class. Actually, it was pretty funny that you threw up on Mr. Papalardi's shoes. We were all cracking up about it."

I stared at her and couldn't talk.

"It's no big deal to throw up in class," she said. "Everybody does it some time or other. I never did it, but Mary Jane did in third grade." She laughed a weird kind of laugh and Mary Jane turned beet red. "Do you remember that, Mary Jane?" she said. "Tommy Ulster watched her do it and then *he* got sick and he threw up; the whole floor was practically covered---" She looked at the two of us and stopped talking. I think our mouths were wide open.

"I'm real glad you're coming back to school this week," she said. "You should eat with us in the cafeteria. There's room at our table if you want to join us," she said.

I didn't answer; I just stood there trying to smile.

That night I sat up in bed thinking about Lou Ellen and everything that was going on. I was pretty worried about what the kids would say. And then I thought about what Lou Ellen had said about Mary Jane making Tommy Ulster throw up all over the floor. I started laughing thinking about what must have been happening with all of the other kids in the class.

"Are you okay?" my mother asked.

I told her what I was laughing about and at first she said, "EWW!"

Then we got even more hysterical than the night before. When we were through laughing, she said, "I really like Lou Ellen."

"Yeah, she's pretty hot," I said.

CHAPTER 7

At about ten o'clock on the third day Dr. Ellis said I could go home. He said he was proud of our family and that we were ready to handle what needed to be handled.

"That doesn't mean you are all off the hook," he said. "Your work is just starting. You need to make sure you check your sugar and take your insulin faithfully." He looked at me and smiled. "Meg said you gave yourself your first injection like you've been doing it for years. Good job. Do you have any questions?" He looked at all three of us. Then he looked at my mother. "You spoke with the school nurse?"

"Yes," she said. "I'm meeting with her this afternoon to talk about J.J. Meg helped to set up a kit with things he might need at school."

"Good. The nurse there has dealt with my patients before and she knows about diabetes, so

46

you'll be in good hands." He looked back at me. "Are you ready to go back to school?"

I wanted to sound like I wasn't worried, but I was thinking so hard about it, nothing came out of my mouth.

"No one expects you to be a hero, J.J. Do the things you used to do. Everybody has something to deal with. If you do what you know is right for you, you'll be fine. Be sure to carry glucose tabs with you at all times. If you feel a little shaky, you might be having an insulin reaction. Pop one of the tabs and you'll feel fine pretty quickly." He looked at all three of us again. "You're going to be in touch with Meg pretty much every day for a while. We also set up an appointment in my office for next week. If you have any questions at any time, call us. No question is too small, too large, or too silly." He looked directly at me. "Understand?"

"Yeah," I said.

After he left we gathered up all of my things and I said good-bye to everyone I had met there. I thanked all the nurses and went down the elevator with my mother without talking. My father was already in the parking lot getting the car. We were having an April shower. I got in the car and sat quietly in the back seat watching the rain hit the windows and listened to the wipers swish back and forth.

V.T. Dacquino

The next morning was Thursday. I was happy
that I only had two days to deal with before the
weekend. I tested my sugar and it was 100 --- right
in the range where Dr. Ellis and Meg said it should
be. I gave myself my injection with my parents
watching me closely then ate my breakfast. Back in
my room, I thought about what I should wear. I
decided on regular jeans and a plain sweatshirt.

"I can drive you in," my father said when I went
into the kitchen. "I have a light day today."

"Can I take the bus?" I asked. "I don't want to
be dropped off."

He looked a little hurt, but I think he
understood.

"Sure," he said.

They both said good-bye like I was leaving
home forever and it made me ten times more
nervous, but I didn't say anything to them. I gave a
little wave and my mother said, "Wait! Do you
have your glucose tabs in case of an emergency?"

I checked my pocket and said, "Yes," loudly,
then kept walking away without turning back. It
was a little chilly and I was glad I had picked a
sweatshirt to wear.

There were the usual kids at the bus stop, but
none of them said anything about my not having
been there for a few days. The bus driver
mentioned it though. She said it was nice to have
me back.

I sat in the last seat where I usually sit and we picked up a couple kids from class. They looked at me and I knew what they were thinking, but they didn't say anything to me except hi.

When we pulled up in front of the school, Lou Ellen was waiting on the front steps with Mary Jane. She was trying to act like she wasn't there on purpose. I stayed in my seat and let the other kids get off before me; I could tell that she was either getting annoyed or worried that I wasn't on the bus. Just before I got off, the driver said, "The nurse gave me some orange juice to keep on the bus and reminded me that I should pay attention if you say you aren't feeling well. You'll tell me if you aren't feeling well, right?" she asked.

"Yeah, thanks," I said.

Lou Ellen ran right up to me when I stepped off.

"Hi," she said.

"Hi," I answered back.

We walked through the halls together and I told her I had to stop off to see the nurse. When I got there the nurse was pretty happy to see me. She asked me if I had taken my insulin and I told her I did. She said I should come down about 11:15 to check my blood sugar before going to the cafeteria and asked me if I had my lunch and a snack if I needed it. I told her I did. She also said that the teachers had all been to a meeting where they were

49

taught about my diabetes and were instructed to send me out whenever I wasn't feeling right. She said I should never feel funny about needing a snack or testing.

"I have your insulin and meter here for when you need it," she said. "Your mother left it with me with anything else you might need."

When she was through talking, I turned and saw Lou Ellen and Mary Jane waiting in the doorway, listening.

"I can walk down here with you at lunch time," she said.

"I think I'd rather meet you in the cafeteria," I told her.

The kids in the hall were pretty friendly when we got upstairs and Mr. Papalardi slapped me five as soon as he saw me. "Hey, buddy. Welcome home. How are you feeling?"

"Fine," I said. I couldn't help looking down at his shoes. They were new.

None of the kids made a big deal out of anything but I could tell they were dying to ask me questions. We got up to say the Pledge of Allegiance and I pulled out my books for class. The room got quiet and I nearly jumped out of my skin when Mr. Papalardi called out my name. "I believe this is yours," he said.

He was holding out something in his hand. I went up to get it and smiled when I saw the 97% on the top of my social studies test. I laughed to myself because I didn't even remember I had finished it.

"Nice work," he said.

When I got back to the desk, a little yellow note was sitting there with "To JJ" written on it.

I opened it and it said,

JJ

"Don't forget to sit at our table for lunch. What did you get on your test?"

Lou Ellen

I turned her note over and wrote on the back:

"I got a 97."

JJ.

A minute later, Tony, the kid behind me, tapped me on my back and handed me another note.

♩♩

"Cool. I only got an 89%. See you at lunch."

Lou Ellen

At 11:10, the bell rang. I got to the nurse by 11:15. She took out a box with my name on it and I took out the meter and did a finger stick. My blood sugar was 75.

It's a little low," she said. Do you keep glucose tabs on you?"

"Yes," I said.

"Well, for now," she said, "take one of these. It serves the same purpose." She took a Chuckles candy out of my kit and said, "This will keep you from getting lower while you're waiting to eat. Do you have your lunch?"

I held up my bag and she smiled.

"If you need to come down at all before school ends, don't hesitate. It's going to take a little while to get to know what works best for you. I'll be here if you need me."

Lou Ellen was at her table. I felt funny going over to it; there were all girls there. They said hi and I waved, but I couldn't do it. I walked right by her and went to my usual table. I emptied my lunch bag without looking up and there wasn't much in it. I had a bag of potato chips, a bottle of water, a turkey sandwich and an apple. I ate with my head down, and when I looked up, Lou Ellen wasn't at her table. But someone *was* sitting at mine.

CHAPTER 8

T ony Comabella was sitting at the end of my table and he sort of waved when I looked at him. Tony sits behind me in social studies and he's the one who passes my notes back to Lou Ellen. I don't really know him because he only came to our school last year and doesn't say very much. I only know that some of the girls like him and try to sit next him.

"How's it going?" he asked.

"Things are okay," I said. I didn't know how else to answer him. Why was he suddenly talking to me? And why was he sitting at my table? I tried to think of where he used to sit during lunch, but I couldn't remember. He didn't talk again for a while and I tried to not look at him, but then he said, "I have it too."

"What?" I asked.

He grabbed up his food and slid in closer to my end of the table so that we were directly across from each other. "I have diabetes, too. I was diagnosed when I was eight."

I just stared at him.

"It's not a big deal if you take care of it," he said.

I was still too shocked to say anything and he reached for his sandwich and bit into it. "I don't really talk about it," he said with his mouth full, "but Mr. Papalardi said I should tell you about me."

Just then, Mr. Papalardi showed up. "Hey, guys. I'm glad to see you're together."

I don't know what got into me, but I felt my temper rising. Who did Mr. Papalardi think he was? What right did he have to talk about me to the other kids?

"I think you should mind your own business," I said to him. "I don't really need your help."

I pulled my chair back and got up. My food was still on the table but I didn't feel like eating anymore. "Hey, wait a minute," Mr. Papalardi said. "Can we talk?"

I glanced behind me as I raced out of the cafeteria, but he wasn't there. At first I was going to leave the school and go for a walk, but I knew that would only get me into trouble. I went to math class and sat there trying not to be angry. Lou Ellen, Mary Jane, and Tony were in all my afternoon classes but I didn't look at any of them.

55

At the end of the day, Mr. Papalardi was in the hall by my locker. "Can I talk to you for a minute before you leave?" he asked.

"I'll miss my bus," I said.

"I just want to apologize, J. I was trying to do what I thought was right and wasn't thinking enough about how you might feel about it. I only knew that you were having a real hard time and I was trying to make things better for you. Some of the kids were concerned about you and were asking questions; I felt I had to tell them the truth so they wouldn't imagine worse things and start spreading rumors. I didn't want them rushing up to you when you got back to ask you a million questions and put you on the spot. I'm sorry that it was the wrong thing for you."

I know he would have liked me to say it was okay, but I couldn't.

"I have to get on my bus," I said.

He nodded a yes and I went to catch up with the rest of the kids. Lou Ellen, Mary Jane, nor Tony is on my bus so I didn't have to deal with them. But I *did* have to deal with *me*, and I hated myself and my diabetes.

I wasn't feeling great by supper time, and my count was low. I was sitting on my bed feeling shaky. My father made me tell him why I hadn't eaten lunch.

"It's not a good enough reason," he said. "You can't let things like that interfere with your control, J. I'll talk to Mr. Papalardi---"

Maybe it was because I was feeling so lousy, but I yelled at him. "No! Why can't you all just leave me alone? It's my life, and if I don't want to take care of myself; it's my own business!"

"J, that's not true---"

My mother came into the room and asked what was wrong, and my father stopped talking. He had been sitting on my bed next to me and got up. My mother signaled him with her head to leave and then winked at him the way she's good at doing and came to sit next to me.

"I don't want to talk about it," I said.

"I hope you didn't think all of this was going to be easy," she said.

I didn't answer.

"What happened in school today?"

I still didn't answer.

"Okay," she said. "We need to give you your injection and then we'll have supper. You don't have to talk about anything you don't want to talk about."

At bedtime, I just lay there thinking, and thinking, and decided what I was going to do.

****

V.T. Dacquino

The next morning, I rushed to my locker and went into Mr. Papalardi's room early. He was writing something on the board and looked nervous when he saw me.

"Hey, J," he said. "I---"

"It's okay," I told him. "But I don't want you to talk about it or mention it in front of the other kids again."

He looked like he wanted to hug me or something, and I was glad when he didn't.

"You have a deal," he said "this has been a real case of the student teaching the teacher."

I was feeling okay, so I said, "Well, you get a C-."

He smiled a pretty big smile and said, "I'll try harder next time."

The bell hadn't rung yet so I went back out to my locker. Tony's locker is about five down from mine and I said hi to him. He looked pretty surprised.

"Hi," he said.

About ten minutes after class started, Tony tapped me on the shoulder and handed me a little yellow note:

Dear J.J.

It's okay that you didn't sit with me and you don't have to come to my party if you don't want to.

Lou Ellen Parker

I turned the note over and wrote.

Lou Ellen,

I still want come to your party. Thank you for visiting me in the hospital.

JJ

I turned in my seat and gave the note to Tony. A few minutes later, he tapped my shoulder and handed me another one of Lou Ellen's notes. All it said was:

"Great! You're welcome."

I turned to look at her and she was smiling a kind of shy smile. I turned and looked at the note again and this time I noticed something written on the back. It was in a different handwriting:

If you want to go to the PIZZA
PALACE after school sometime, we
can go together. We can just get a diet
soda or something.

Tony

I turned and looked at Tony without even
thinking about it and said. "If you want to sit at my
table again for lunch today we can talk about it."

"Sure," he said.

"Is there something I should know about?" Mr.
Papalardi asked from the front of the room.

"No," I said. I must have said it pretty weird
because a lot of the kids laughed.

At lunch I went to the nurse and did my thing
and then went right to my table in the cafeteria and
looked over at Lou Ellen's table. She was with her
friends and didn't wave for me to come over or
anything, which was real cool because I was afraid
she was going to call me over to sit with her. I took
out my sandwich, chips, and drink and Tony came
up and sat down.

"How's it going?" he asked

"It's going good," I said. "I'm sorry about---"

"It's okay," he interrupted, "You don't have to go to the Palace with me if you don't want to. I just---"

"That's okay," I said. "I've never really gone there without my parents. We get pizza there for dinner a lot."

"I go there after school almost every day," he said. "My parents work in the city and they don't get home until about 6:30. I go there or the library until they get home."

"Wow," I said, "that's cool." Only I didn't really think it was cool. I was pretty glad that my mother was home when I got there. "I just would have to let my mother know that I was not taking the bus from school. She or my father would probably want to pick me up when we were done."

"Do you want to go today?" he asked.

I was going to say that I would call and ask if it would be okay, but we were interrupted by Mary Jane and a little *pink* note. It was to Tony!

Dear Tony,

Lou Ellen is having a birthday party on June 7 and JJ is invited. She said to tell you that you are also invited if you would like to come.

Mary Jane

Tony handed the note to me and I looked up at him real quick; he made this weird face and then the two of us just cracked up laughing.

CHAPTER 9

"**I**'m only having diet soda," I told my mother on the phone.

"But we don't even know him," my mother said. "Why don't we come there and meet him; your father and I will have a slice of pizza or something at another table."

"Forget it," I said. "I just won't go."

I looked over at Tony and I knew he had heard me. He looked real disappointed.

"Hang on a minute," my mother said. I know she had her hand over the receiver because I couldn't hear anything she was saying. After a couple of minutes, my father was on the line.

"J, we're a little nervous because it's the first time you asked to do something like this, but we're glad you're going. Give us a call when you're ready to come home and we'll come to get you. Order a large cheese pizza-to-go for us for supper.

Tell Rico, the owner, that it's for me and I'll pay him for it when I pick it up."

"Thanks, Dad," I said. I smiled over at Tony and gave him the "thumbs-up" signal. He raised his arms and said, "YES!"

Pizza Palace is less than three blocks from the school. It's sort of divided into two parts. One side is a restaurant that's mostly for adults and families; the other side is for take-outs, slices, and sandwiches. Kids from the high school are allowed to go there for lunch and some of them hang out there after school. The pizza's great and there are never any problems with fights or drugs.

Kids from both the middle and high school were hanging out by the curb when we got there and some of the kids from my class were outside, too. I think they were pretty surprised to see me show up there.

We passed through a small crowd by the front door and I figured the inside would be packed since there were so many kids outside, but the inside was almost empty. There was a small table off in the corner and Tony went right to it. Rico, the owner, knew Tony and said hi to him from over the counter, and then he recognized me. "How's your dad doing?" he asked me. "Is he home writing his books?"

"I think so," I said. "He told me to say hi to you and order a large cheese pizza to go for him. He's coming to pick me up."

"No problem," he said. "I'll wait a little while before I put it in. You guys want slices and something to drink?"

Tony ordered two diet cokes and said we might have slices later.

Suddenly, I thought about something! How was I supposed to pay for my soda? I was broke. Tony must have seen me reach for my pocket or noticed the look on my face, because he said, "I can pay for it. My parents give me a lot of money for eating out and I never spend it all. You can pay some other time."

"I wasn't planning on going anywhere after school," I said. "My father will pay you back when he comes."

"That's cool," he answered, and then he changed the subject. "I really like this place. It reminds me of where I used to live."

"Was it near here?" I asked.

"No," he said. He seemed sad and didn't say anything for a few minutes. Rico came over with our drinks and asked if we had changed our minds about the slices yet. We both said no.

"I used to live Upstate," Tony continued. "All of my cousins lived near us and there were a lot of kids on my block. My parents moved their law firm to Manhattan."

"They're both lawyers?"

"Yeah," he said. "Do your parents work in Manhattan?"

"No," I said. "My father works at home and my mother works as his assistant. She helps set up his appearances and handles his book sales. He's a writer and lecturer."

"Is that what Rico meant when he said, 'Is your father home writing books'? Does he write books?"

I was wondering if I should tell him about my father's book, and then I just said it. "He wrote *KISS THE CANDY GOOD-BYE* about a kid with diabetes."

He looked shocked and then said, "Are you serious? I read that book. I love that book. The librarian from my other school gave it to me to read when she found out I had diabetes. I still have a copy of it at home. I felt like I knew the main character, Jimmy James---" He stopped talking and looked at me with a weird expression, "Is your name J.J. because---?"

"It could have been worse," I said. "He could have named me after Jimmy James' best friend Margaret"

Tony cracked up laughing. "Yeah, I guess JJ is a better name for you than Margaret," he said finally. And then he started laughing again.

He was quiet for another little while and said, "I really like reading. My father thinks I'm trying to read every book in the library."

"Reading's all right," I said.

"When I found out what I had, I read everything I could about it. Have you been reading up on diabetes? I have tons of stuff on it if you want to borrow it. I felt bad for you when Mr. Papalardi told me about you."

I felt my anger rising. "Did your teacher at your old school tell everyone in your class about you?" I asked.

"No, it was different for me than it was for you. I was in third grade and I didn't have any of the symptoms in school. Besides, my teacher wasn't as cool as Mr. Papalardi." He stopped talking and looked up at me. "Do you think that Mr. Papalardi told the whole class about your diabetes? He didn't, you know. I stayed after the day you got sick and asked him about you. He said he didn't know for sure and then the next day after school he told me and Mary Jane and Lou Ellen because he knew we really wanted to know. He knows Lou Ellen likes you and he knew I would understand because I have it. He told us not to say anything to the other kids. After Lou Ellen and Mary Jane left, I asked him if I should talk to you about it and he said I should." He stopped talking again and looked embarrassed or something. "That's not why I tried to make friends with you," he said. "I liked you before that because you aren't like some of the other kids. You're a lot like the friends I have at camp."

"Camp?" I said.

"Yeah, in the summer when we aren't in school I go to stay with my grandmother back home and then I go to a camp for kids with diabetes. It's called The Circle of Life Camp."

"Everyone there has diabetes?" I asked.

"Yeah," he said. "But it's not like that's the only thing everyone there thinks about. It's more like you *don't* think about it because everyone has it. Even the counselors and the founder have diabetes."

I was going to ask him more about it, but I heard someone shouting from behind me. "Oh, wow. Hi, Tony. Hi, J.J."

Lou Ellen was standing there with her whole pack of girlfriends.

"I can't believe you're here. Come and sit with us," she said.

I looked from one gawking face to the other and almost felt like sliding under my table. Somehow, though, it didn't seem as bad sitting at a table with them with Tony there. I looked at him and he shook his head yes.

"Don't buy anything more to drink or eat," Lou Ellen said. "We're ordering two cheese pizzas and a pitcher of soda. You can share with us."

I was about to say I wasn't hungry or thirsty, but she came over and whispered in my ear loud enough for the whole place to hear. "It's diet."

She didn't wait for an answer. She took my arm and led me to her table. Tony followed us and sat in the empty chair next to Lou Ellen. Then she "whispered" into my ear again, "Can you eat pizza?"

"I'm not very hungry right now," I whispered loudly. She gave me a look like she was saying, it's okay I won't give away your secret.

When the pizza came, she offered a slice to Tony. He took it right away, said thanks, and bit into it.

I watched Tony eat and was real tempted to ask for a slice. It smelled amazingly good and I figured if he could do it, so could I; everyone else was eating slices, too, although that didn't stop most of the girls from talking. I was wondering who was listening if everyone was talking at the same time. Just as I was about to say I wanted a slice, Lou Ellen said, "This table is so crowded. Why don't the four of us move to your smaller table over there?"

She and Mary Jane moved to the new seats and Tony and I followed. She didn't bring any of the

V.T. Dacquino

pizza with her and I guess I was glad. I didn't want to get tempted. "Tony, did you get a chance to answer Mary Jane's note yet?" Lou Ellen asked. "I hope you're coming to my birthday party on June 7."

"Sure," he said. "I'll come."

"It's going to be awesome," she said. "We're going to have all kinds of great games." She looked over at Mary Jane when she said that and the two of them started blushing and giggling.

I had a good hunch she *wasn't* talking about games like "Pin-the-tail-on the Donkey."

Things were going along pretty well. Tony turned out to be a lot less quiet and shy than I thought he was. The girls were laughing and giggling at things he was saying and the more they laughed, the funnier he got.

And then this real sick feeling came over me. What had I been thinking! This was the first time I was out with kids after school and my father was picking me up like I was in third grade or something. I started worrying about things like what he would be wearing and if he would say anything stupid. I was really glad he had ordered the pizza because he at least had an excuse for being there. And then he walked in.

Most of the kids that had been by the curb were hungry now and at their tables eating.

"Hey," my father said when he saw us. "How are you guys doing?"

He was wearing a light-blue pull-over shirt and jeans and there wasn't anything too abnormal about the way he looked.

Lou Ellen and Mary Jane were pretty glad to see him and Tony stood up with his hand out. I could tell by my father's face that he was pretty impressed with Tony's offering to shake his hand.

"I read your book," Tony said. "I really liked it."

"I'm glad to hear that you're a reader," my father said. "Readers are leaders."

I looked quickly over at everyone's expression. Readers are leaders! That sounded like something a teacher would say to little kids. But they were all looking at him and were really paying attention to everything he was saying.

"Hey, what's happening?" Rico said to my father from the counter. "I have your pie ready for you."

My father walked over and talked to Rico and Tony said my father was "cool." The girls all agreed with him and I was pretty relieved, but I was thinking that Tony could have said anything to those girls and they would have agreed.

When my father got back to the tables, he said that he had paid for our sodas and would have paid for the girls' food too if they hadn't paid already.

71

They said thank you anyway and he asked if anybody needed a ride.

"My father's picking me up," Lou Ellen said. "He's picking up pizza for dinner." Everyone looked down at the pizza my father was holding and just laughed. Then my father asked Tony if he wanted a ride home.

"It's not that far," he said, "but sure, I'll take a ride."

We said good-bye to the girls and nobody said anything about it being the weekend and not seeing each other tomorrow. Just as we got to the car, Lou Ellen ran up to me and handed me a yellow note and ran back inside.

Tony laughed with me and I opened it. It said

JJ,

You can call me over the weekend if you want. Remember, my number is 242-7707.

Lou Ellen Parker

And then Mary Jane came out and handed a pink note to Tony. It said exactly the same thing, only it had Tony's and Mary Jane's names on it and Mary Jane's phone number. We got hysterical laughing and my father was laughing just as hard, only we never told him what was so funny.

I decided to get in the back seat so Tony could sit next to me, but when I started to get in the car, I noticed that Tony wasn't following me. He was watching some guy in a black car with tinted windows drive by us. The expression on his face was weird, like he was scared of something.

"Hey," I said. "Get in."

"I think I'm going to walk," he said. "I forgot. It's still early and my parents are probably not home yet. Thanks anyway."

"Are you sure?" I said.

"Yeah," he said. "I'm sure."

I told my father to hold on a minute and wrote down my phone number. "Give me a call this weekend if you aren't doing anything. Maybe we can get together. Is everything all right?"

"Yeah, it's fine," he said. And then he just walked away looking toward the black car parked at the far end of the street.

CHAPTER 10

When we got home, I changed out of my school clothes and tested my blood sugar. I was starving. I wrote down my count in my log book and gave myself my injection. When everything was put away, I rushed to the table and grabbed the biggest slice of pizza in the box.

"You're acting like you haven't eaten before," my father said. "Why didn't you eat anything at Pizza Palace? How was your blood sugar?"

"It was fine," I said. "I just didn't want to spoil dinner."

"You shouldn't deprive yourself of things you want," my mother said. "You just need to carb count the way Meg taught you and take your insulin."

"I'm fine. Can I just eat now?" I said.

I know I sounded annoyed and my father looked like he was going to say something, but my mother gave him her look.

After dinner, I went to my room and tried to think about what was going on with Tony. Why had he been so worried about the black car? I knew my father hadn't notice it, or he would have said something. I almost thought I should talk to him about it, and then I figured it was just my imagination. What I needed to worry about was what I was going to do all weekend. I reached into my pocket and took out Lou Ellen's note and stared at her phone number for a few minutes. It was about 6:30. I picked up the phone and started dialing; I got all the way up to the last seven in her number before I hung up fast.

On the next try, I didn't even make it to the first seven in her phone number. What would I say to her? Would she be glad I called? Maybe it was still too early to call.

I was just about to go into the living room when the phone rang.

"JJ?" my mother called.

"Yeah," I said.

"It's for you. Pick up," she said.

I went to my bedroom phone and lifted the receiver quickly.

"This is Mr. Papalardi," Tony said in a deep voice. "I'm checking to see if you are doing your homework."

"Wow! You sound exactly like him," I said.

"I *do*?" he asked

"Not even close," I said. We both laughed and he asked what I was doing.

"Nothing. I finished eating a little while ago and now I'm just hanging around." I thought for a minute and said, "Is everything okay? You seemed a little spooked out when you saw that black car go by us."

"I didn't see a black car," he said. "I'm fine. I called to see what you're doing."

"Do you want to come over? I know my parents wouldn't mind if you came over. Or I could even come over there."

He paused for a long time and said, "I guess I might be able to come over there. My parents don't really like me bringing friends home when they aren't here."

"I thought you said they get home at 6:30," I said.

He paused again.

"On Fridays they go to dinner in the city and get home late. We have an au pair from France who stays with me when they aren't here. She knows I don't like being with her so she let's me go out as long as I tell her where I'm going and who I'm going with."

"*What* do you have from France?" I asked.

"An au pair. She's like a housekeeper who's an expert on diabetes; she's a student at the university and earns room and board by taking care of things when my parents aren't around. So do you want me to come over?"

"Sure," I said. "But I have to ask my parents first. Hang on."

My father and mother came into my room together when I called to them and they were happy about Tony coming over. They asked if his parents were dropping him off.

"They aren't home," I said.

"Who is he home with?" my mother asked.

"His au pair," I said. "Do you know what that is?"

My mother raised her eyebrows and my father said, "Yes, we do. We'll need to talk with her."

"What?" I said.

"We can't just have him come over here without permission. I need to know that she's okay with it. We would expect the same thing from them if you were going there," my father said. "Ask him if we can talk with her."

I put the receiver back to my ear, but all I heard was a dial tone.

I wanted to call him back, but I couldn't; I didn't have his number. I checked the caller I.D., but all it said was, "Private Caller"

****

I sat up on my bed thinking about what was going on with Tony and it was driving me crazy. My parents said I couldn't go over there to ask him what was up, and besides I didn't even know where he lived.

"There's obviously something going on," my mother said. "My guess is that he didn't get permission to come over and was trying to come over anyway. You're going to have to wait until he calls you again. We shouldn't try to make any more assumptions since we don't really know him or his family."

At 7:30 I couldn't stand hanging around in my room anymore. I picked up the phone and dialed 242-7707.

A man's voice answered. "Parker residence."

"Hello. May I speak with Lou Ellen Parker?"

"May I ask who is calling?"

"This is JJ Johnson. I'm her friend from school."

"Hang on a minute," he said. He was gone a pretty long time and then Lou Ellen picked up.

"Hello?"

"Lou Ellen? This is JJ. Is it all right that I called?"

"Of course it's all right," she said. "Why do you think I gave you my number? I was really surprised to see you at Pizza Palace today? Were you glad you came?"

"Yeah," I said.

"Tony is really nice. Are you going to see him at all this weekend?"

I was deciding whether to tell her what had happened and then decided not to do it.

"JJ? Are you there?"

"Huh? Yeah, I'm here. I don't know if I'll see him. I don't really know him very well."

"Yeah, isn't it weird that he finally started talking? Mary Jane has kind of liked him for a while but he didn't talk very much or hang out with anyone until now." She paused for a minute. "He was sort of like someone else I know."

"Who?" I asked. And then I felt like a jerk because I realized she was talking about me. Luckily, she laughed and thought I was teasing her.

"Did you get to see his house?" she asked. "Isn't it huge?"

"You saw his house?" I asked her.

"Yeah," she said. "One day after school Mary Jane and I followed him home. He lives in a huge mansion with tall white pillars on the front porch. Didn't you see it when you dropped him off?"

"We didn't drop him off," I said. "He changed his mind about the ride when we got to the car."

I didn't think I should say anything about the black car or the phone call so I just kept quiet.

"JJ? Are you there? I keep losing you."

"It must be the phone," I said.

"What are you doing tomorrow?" she asked. "Maybe we can go to the Pizza Palace for lunch or go to the park or something."

I was about to say I'd have to ask my parents, but it sounded babyish. I just said, "Sure, what time?"

"About noon. We can meet right at Pizza Palace. I'll invite Mary Jane. If you talk to Tony maybe you can ask him to come, too. "

"*If* I talk to him," I said, but I had a strange feeling that Tony wasn't going to call back tonight.

CHAPTER 11

My parents were pretty happy that I was going to the Pizza Palace with Lou Ellen and Mary Jane. They said I could ask Rico to use his phone if I wasn't feeling right. My father offered to take me there, but he knew I would rather walk.

"Remember that you need to have something to eat for lunch," my mother said, "and be home before supper. You need to check your sugar around two."

I looked into her face and said, "Can I go now?"

She smiled. "Yes, you can go now."

Lou Ellen and Mary Jane were already sitting at our table for four in Pizza Palace and they jumped up when they saw me. Rico noticed me too and said hello the minute I walked in.

"I'm glad you got here," he said. "These girls were driving me crazy."

"We were not," Lou Ellen said.

Rico made a "That's-your-opinion," face and laughed. "Should I throw in a cheese slice for you?" he asked.

"Yes," I said. "And I'll have a diet soda." I could see the girls already had their slices and sodas. Lou Ellen looked up at me and I knew what she wanted to ask before she asked it.

"Yes, I can have pizza," I said. "I can have everything you can have."

"I know," she said. "I've been reading about diabetes on line. I learned all about what it is and what you have to do to take care of it. You want to know what I learned?"

"No," I said.

She looked at me to see if I was joking, and when she knew I wasn't, she said, "Did you talk to Tony at all?"

"No," I said.

She waited a minute, like she hadn't planned what she was about to say, and said, "Mary Jane had an idea. Let's go to Tony's and walk by his house. Maybe he'll see us and come out." She stopped and looked at Mary Jane. "Or maybe we can just walk up and ring his doorbell."

I stared at her and thought about going to Tony's house. What if he got mad at us for going there? But I also was dying to see his house. Maybe he would be happy to see us. Maybe he would run out and invite us in. But what if the guy in the black car was a kidnapper or something and something bad happened to Tony? Suppose we noticed a clue that could help us to save him?

"Did you know that you look real scary when you're thinking?" Lou Ellen asked. "It's like you go off to another world or something."

"Before you go to any other worlds," Rico said from behind us, "Here's your pizza and soda."

I took my slice from him, thanked Rico, and said, "We can walk by, but I don't think we should ring his doorbell."

****

We headed down Main Street and I still wasn't sure if we were doing the right thing. Lou Ellen and Mary Jane talked a mile a minute and I kept checking the streets. I was hoping to run into Tony.

After a couple of blocks, Lou Ellen said, "This is the turn. He lives right on this street."

I should have known. We were on the Esplanade. Every house on the block was bigger than the one before it. Some houses were stone with big circle driveways and tall flowering trees, and some of the houses were wood and covered in ivy. None of them looked alike the way they did in my neighborhood.

"Oh, wow," she said. "There's the house—and there's Tony!"

We ducked behind a stone lion's head that bordered one of the driveways and looked down the block at one of the biggest houses in the village. It had tall white pillars like the White House in Washington and a huge front lawn and circular driveway. In the center of the driveway was the black car with the tinted windows! A young muscular guy was helping to load stuff into it and Tony was standing there with a suitcase in each hand.

Mary Jane grabbed my arm and nearly scared me to death. "Is he going somewhere?" I turned to look at her quickly because she almost never spoke to me.

"It looks that way," Lou Ellen said.

We watched them for a little while longer while they loaded the car with the things at the curb, and one thing was perfectly clear---they both looked like they were watching for someone--- and hoping they weren't being watched. Then something really weird happened---they shook hands and hugged for a second before the driver got into the car and drove off without Tony!

"Should we go up to him?" Lou Ellen asked.

"No," I said. "We should stop spying on him and leave him alone."

We walked away from his block and went to the park on the far side of the village. There was a playground for little kids there and we swung on the swings for a while, but I wasn't feeling great and was too busy thinking about Tony to enjoy being there. I looked at my watch and it was 3:30; I needed to check my sugar. I didn't want to do it in front of the girls so I suggested that we go to the Pizza Palace. By the time we got there, I felt tired and shaky. Something weird was going on with me and it was making me real scared. My heart was beating out of my chest and my fingers and toes felt all tingly.

There weren't any other customers in the Palace and Rico was twirling dough in the air. He stopped twirling and looked at me. I couldn't really walk very well and sat in one of the booths. "Are you okay?"

"Does he look okay?" Lou Ellen asked. "He has diabetes."

I made myself say, "I'll be all right."

"Do you have candy or glucose tabs?" Lou Ellen asked.

I looked at her, but it was like I couldn't think very fast. I put my hand into my pocket and the tabs were in there. I unwrapped them and popped them into my mouth. After about ten minutes, I felt a little better and asked Rico for a slice of pizza and a soda.

I felt okay enough to get up and went into the bathroom to check my sugar. It was still only 80, but I knew it would go up because of the pizza and

V.T. Dacquino

soda. When I got out of the bathroom, Rico and the girls were standing there staring at me.

"How about we give your dad a call?" Rico said. He handed me the phone and I dialed our number. My father answered and said he would be right over.

"I'm sorry I made you walk so far," Lou Ellen said.

I tried to smile at her. "You didn't make me do anything," I said. "I walked because I wanted to."

My father didn't make a big fuss when he got there. I think he saw that I was feeling okay. We said thank you to Rico and good-bye to the girls and we left. On the way, my father said, "Are you sure you feel okay?"

"Yes," I said.

"Did you check your sugar?"

"I checked it in the bathroom after I ate. It was 80."

"It should go up now that you've eaten. If you're sure you're feeling better," he said, "I want to stop to pick up a little present for all us before we go home."

"I'm okay," I said.

CHAPTER 12

I was pretty excited when we got home because the present my father was talking about was a cell phone.

"You can't always rely on someone having a phone when you need it," my father said. "I think this will give us all peace of mind, as long as you don't abuse it. It's primarily for emergencies. There's a book that comes with it. We bought the plan that has unlimited incoming calls but you need to limit how long you talk to your friends on it. Why don't you rest a while and read up on how to use it? We're going to have supper in a little while. Check your sugar."

I went to my room and did a finger stick. My count was almost 250. I decided to take an extra two units of insulin and go back to my reading before supper.

The cell phone was pretty amazing and I was so caught up in reading and learning about it, I jumped when the house phone rang.

"It's for you," my mother said.

I picked it up and it was exactly who I hoped it would be. "Hi, Lou Ellen," I said.

"Are you okay?"

"I'm fine," I said.

"I was worried."

"I'm fine," I said again. "I got a present from my parents."

"A present?"

"Yeah, a cell phone."

"Wow, cool," she said. "My parents won't let me have one. They think I'll 'abuse' it."

"That's the same word my father used when he gave mine to me," I told her.

"Does that mean I can't have the phone number?" she asked.

"You can have it," I said, and I laughed a little when I said, "But don't abuse it."

I gave her the number and we talked for another little while. We talked about school, and me, and her and her party, and Tony. Only I didn't want to talk about Tony. I felt like there was stuff about him maybe I shouldn't know. When she finally hung up, the phone rang again. For a second I thought it was Lou Ellen calling on my cell phone, but it was the house phone again.

"JJ," my mother called. "It's for you again. You sure have become popular. Don't stay on too long, supper is almost ready."

I picked it up and was ready to make a joke to Lou Ellen about "abusing" the phone when I heard Tony say, "Hello?"

"Tony?"

"Yeah," he said. "I'm sorry about hanging up on you last night. My parents came home and I couldn't stay on the line."

I didn't know what to say to him. I wanted to ask him about this afternoon, but I didn't want him to know we were spying on him.

"Are you busy tonight?" he asked.

"Tonight?"

"I mean like after supper, in a little while. My parents will talk to your parents and tell them it's okay for me to come over there or for you to come over here."

I stood there holding the receiver to my ear like I was a statue or something. I couldn't even answer him, and then I said, "Wait. Don't hang up." I threw the receiver onto my bed and ran into the kitchen to ask my parents. When I got back I said, "Are you there?"

"Yeah," he said. "Can one of your parents get on the line? They said you can come here for a while after supper. They don't want me to come over there because of something that happened this afternoon. I can explain when I see you."

"That's good," he said. "I want to talk with you about some stuff, too. I lied to you about some things."

Our parents talked and I ate fast begging the clock to hurry up and get to 6:30. At exactly 6:29, there was a knock at the door. It was Tony.

"Hey," I said.

"Hey," he answered. He said hello to my parents and I took him downstairs to my room.

"You have a fireplace in your room?" he asked.

"Yeah," I said. "This was supposed to be the family room, but my father designed a bedroom out of it for me."

"That's cool," he said. Then his smile went away and he sat on the edge of my bed. "There are some things I have to tell you," he said.

"You don't have to tell me anything you don't want to," I told him. "Friends don't always have to tell friends everything, do they?"

"I want to," he said. "I lied to you about the au pair girl and not seeing the black car yesterday. We don't have an au pair girl. My father paid a guy named Vinny to be our chauffeur and my body guard and caregiver. He was the guy you saw in our black Lincoln Town Car."

"Why do you need a body guard?"

"My father worries a lot about me because of our money and my parents being away from home so much. He's afraid someone will try to kidnap me or take me for ransom. But he's not going to have to worry about that now."

"What do you mean?"

"My father had to fire Vinny yesterday."

I thought back to Tony in the driveway shaking hands with the guy from the black car and hugging him.

"We're almost broke," he said.

I almost laughed when he said that because I thought he was joking, and then it looked like he was going to cry. "My father invested most of our money with an investor and he robbed us. He robbed a lot of people in a thing called a Ponzi scheme. My father knew him and trusted him with our money."

I stood there staring at him. I was trying to remember a talk my mother and father had about the billionaire who talked people into giving him their money to invest. "Wait," I said. "You still have your big house and isn't the black car yours?"

"Nothing is ours," he said. "We borrowed money from the bank to get all those things. We had money in the stock market to cover the payments for them, only we don't have stocks. It was all a lie. Everything is stolen."

"Can't you get it back? Can't you make him return what he stole from you? They caught him didn't they?"

"My father said it's impossible to get back everything he stole from us. He stole from a lot of people. Everyone is trying to get their money back from him." This time there really were tears on his face. "My father said we are going to have to sell our house and maybe move back near my grandmother Upstate." He started to cry a little harder and I didn't know what to say or do for him. "A lot of it is my fault."

"Your fault?" I said. "How could it be your fault?"

"I prayed that something would happen so that I could spend more time with my parents. I made it happen."

I looked at him trying to think of what to tell him. "I don't think prayers work that way," I said. "I think the person responsible is the guy who stole your parents' money."

He sat there quietly, and then said, "Anyway. My parents said I can probably finish out the school year here, but then we have to move."

"Can you still go to the camp for kids with diabetes?"

He looked up quickly and wiped his face with his sleeve. "I don't know," he said. "If I can, can you?"

"Maybe," I said. "Tell me more about it."

Tony and I talked for a long time. I told him about what happened to me and how we went to his house and saw him with Vinny. We talked about the girls and school and when we were young and about both having diabetes. We said it was weird that we became friends right at the time we both needed one.

"If you are going to be here until the end of the year, you'll be able to go to Lou Ellen's birthday party," I said, "with Mary Jane."

He looked up at me. His eyes were still red but he had a huge smile on his face. "I think they're going to have kissing games there," he said.

CHAPTER 13

By the time June came around, Tony's news got better. His father hired Vinny back as their chauffer but cut his hours back. Tony convinced his father that he didn't have to worry about him as much any more because he spent so much time with me now. We were almost like brothers; we were together so much, there wasn't time to hang around with Lou Ellen and Mary Jane or be on the streets alone. And my mother and father almost fell off their chairs when they found out Tony had diabetes.

"That's not funny," my father said, when I told him. He honestly thought I was kidding with him. And when I told him about the camp Tony went to he said he would check it out. When he did, he said, "That camp has a great reputation and it's very affordable. I think it would be terrific if you guys could go there together." Lou Ellen made us crack up laughing because she wanted to pretend she had diabetes and sneak into the camp... especially when she found out that girls go there too.

"I'm going," she said.

Tony told her to "F'get about it! Besides," he said, "diabetes is something you can be thankful you don't have."

I looked at him when he said that. Those were the same words my father had said to me. The weirdest thing was that the day I was diagnosed with diabetes was the exact day that some real good things started happening in my life.

On June 7, Lou Ellen was a wreck. All of the plans for her party were set. Her parents set up decorations in the basement and hired a DJ to play music; Rico made all of the food, even little pizzas for every table. I sat at the table with Lou Ellen, Mary Jane, and Tony; Lou Ellen made all the guys wear ties, including me and Tony.

"Stop complaining," Lou Ellen said. "I think you look nice in a tie. At least I didn't force you to wear jackets." Tony and I made faces at each other.

Lou Ellen and Mary Jane were in dresses and Lou Ellen looked amazing. Her hair was pulled back and her dress was sleeveless and short, which was a pretty good thing since it was about a hundred degrees out. Fortunately, the basement was air conditioned.

About twenty kids came, mostly from our school, and some of Lou Ellen's cousins came, too. No adults were allowed downstairs except to check up on us once in a while. When the music finally started, I was pretty surprised; Tony was the first one dancing. Every girl in there was watching him and that *wasn't* a surprise---he was great.

"Where did you learn to dance?" I asked.

"At camp," he said. "You'll learn, too. The dance is the best part of the camp, but don't tell Lou Ellen or we'll really have a hard time keeping her away. At camp we call kids like Lou Ellen "wanna-be's.""

Just then Lou Ellen grabbed my hand and pulled me up to dance.

I didn't lie; I told her the truth. "I don't know how to dance."

"Just move to the music," she said.

I stood there for a minute and looked around at everyone else. Some of them weren't very good and I figured I could fake it better than they could. I started moving my hips to the beat and Tony said, "Hey, I thought you couldn't dance?"

We danced about five fast dances in a row and then a real slow song came on. Tony put his arms around Mary Jane and danced with her. Lou Ellen said, "Ahem."

I tried to copy what Tony was doing without lifting my feet too much. I didn't want to step on

Lou Ellen's feet. My arms felt great around her and she snuggled up close to my body. It made me feel real nervous at first, and then it felt better and better. I couldn't believe I was actually dancing.

After the food and cake, Lou Ellen opened her presents, but Tony and I said she couldn't open our present until everybody left. We got her a joke gift and it would have been totally embarrassing if she had opened it in front of everyone.

"Why can't I open it?" she asked.

"Because it's special," Tony said. "You know, *special,*" he whispered.

Lou Ellen blushed and Mary Jane giggled.

After the presents, some of the kids started to leave and the DJ packed up his things. The only people left were Tony and I and the girls. "We're going to clean up and stay down here for a while," Lou Ellen told her parents, and she closed the door behind them.

The first thing she did was run for our present and started tearing the paper off. Tony and I were trying not to crack up laughing. When she got it open, she stared at it for a minute and showed it to Mary Jane and the two of them roared with laughter: it was a heavy silver picture frame like the one she had given me in the hospital, with an autographed picture of Tony and me in cheerleading uniforms, smiling. It said "Happy Birthday, Lou Ellen" written in black Scripto pen.

When she was through laughing, she said, "I love it." Then she reached over and kissed my cheek.

"Hey, what about me?" Tony asked. "I'm in the picture, too."

She laughed and kissed his cheek and then said, "It's time to play Truth or Dare."

"I've never played it before," I said. "I don't even know how."

"It's simple," Lou Ellen said.

She pulled out a sheet of paper and read the directions:

Get the players into a group, sitting on the floor or around a table. Choose one player to start the game. The player asks "Truth or Dare?" of a second player in the circle. The player chooses between answering a question and performing a dare. Ask the question or present the dare. Ideally, both the questions and the dares should be mildly embarrassing, but not mean or dangerous. Remember, your turn to answer or perform will come around soon. Continue the game by having the person who last told the truth or did the dare ask "Truth or Dare?" of another player.

"This sounds pretty dangerous," Tony said. "What's the point?"

"Well," Lou Ellen said, "The point is to get to know each other better."

"I bet," Tony said. "Who goes first?"

"Me of course," Lou Ellen answered, "I'm the birthday girl." She sat back in her chair and looked at me and then she looked at the door to the upstairs.

"Truth or dare?"

I thought about it for a minute and said, "Truth."

She looked disappointed, and then she said, "Okay. What are you most afraid of?"

I thought again and said, "I'm afraid of playing games like Truth or Dare."

"Why?" she said.

"Hey," Tony said. "I didn't hear anything about asking why in the rules!"

"Yeah, neither did I," I said.

"Okay, fine," she said. "JJ has to ask me now."

I looked at her and said, "Truth or dare?"

She didn't even think about it. She just said, "Dare."

I didn't think about it either. I couldn't believe I said, "I dare you to kiss me on the lips."

All three of them sat there staring at me, and then Lou Ellen said, "Okay."

She came to my side of the table and leaned into me and I closed my eyes and let my lips touch hers.

It was amazing. They were soft and warm and chills were going up my back. But it didn't last very long. A voice from behind us said, "I think we've had enough birthday party for today." Her father came over and escorted me and Tony to the door.

CHAPTER 14

Tony called Vinny on my cell phone and he came to pick us up. He's young and cool and I was a little embarrassed when he told Vinny what had happened. He just laughed and shook his head.

Just as they dropped me off, Lou Ellen called my cell phone. "I can't talk," she said. "My father's furious. I got grounded as soon as you left the house. Don't call here and I can't call you for a while. My father said I have to go directly home after school every day until graduation. 'Maybe', he said, 'you could see each other during the summer, but not until you learn what is and isn't appropriate behavior.' Besides, he said we have to study for our exams. Uh, oh I have to go, he's coming."

She hung up fast and I stood there in front of my house wishing I could be with her. When I walked in, I was sad and trying not to look too guilty. My parents were watching TV and I hoped I could walk by them without being noticed.

"Oh," my father said when he saw me. "You're home." Then he stood up. "Do you have something to tell us?"

"Well---I---"

"What are you nervous about?" he said. "Your mother and I discussed it, and we think it's very healthy. It shows you're growing up right. You're maturing and we're proud of you."

"You are?" I asked. I was trying to figure out how he knew about me and Lou Ellen already. And I couldn't believe he was happy about it. "Did you get a call?" I asked quietly.

"No," he said. "We got it in the mail."

I thought I was having some kind of a bad dream, until he held up something in his hand.

"Look what came today," my father said.

It was a brochure from the camp and I almost burst out laughing.

"That's great," I said. "It's really great."

"It is," my mother said. "We're pleased that you're excited about it and are willing to learn more about your diabetes. And it's great that you gave them our address to send the application."

What I wanted to say was, "Thank you, Tony," because I was sure he was the one who gave the camp our address.

"Why don't you take the brochure into your room and look it over. Your mother and I will fill out the application and write a check out for the deposit. We'll mail it out tomorrow. How was the party?"

"The party was great," I said, and brought the brochure into my room. When I closed the door--- I cracked up laughing. I couldn't wait to tell Tony how I thought they knew I had kissed Lou Ellen. And then I thought of the kiss. It was so great touching my lips to hers--- but I also remembered the tone of her father's voice, and the look on his face.

The brochure from the camp listed all of the things that they do there. It even had photographs, but they got me thinking. Some of them were of the camp's variety "skits." I wasn't so sure I liked that part. There was no way they were going to get me to dress up in any of the weird costumes some of those kids were wearing in the photos and do stuff in front of an audience. And kids were in bathing suits. What was Tony going to say when he knew I was a terrible swimmer? Then, an even worse thing hit me: this was going to be the first time I was ever going to sleep away from home. The camp was over two hours away from my house. What if I got home-sick? What if something went wrong? I didn't even know anyone there but Tony. But that was good wasn't it? Tony would never let anything happen to me. But what could he do? He was only six months older than me. He did know about diabetes, though; everybody there knows about diabetes. What could happen to me that they wouldn't know about?

Suddenly, I wasn't so sure about going.

What I was also thinking was that Lou Ellen might meet someone else while I was at camp.

I called Tony on my cell phone from my room and told him that the brochure had come.

"Great," he said. "Once you send in the deposit there's no turning back. It's good-bye Mom and Dad and hello being away from home."

"Yeah," I said.

"Are you okay?" he asked.

"Sure," I said. "What was that stuff about skits? Does everyone act in them?"

"Absolutely," he said, "we all get to make fools out of ourselves and be ridiculous. You should have seen the skit I was in last year."

"Does everybody go swimming, too?"

"Absolutely," he said. "We get to swim for hours. And the kids who don't know how to swim very well go in the shallow beginner's part for lessons so they don't get in our way of having fun. We call them 'little dippers.'"

Great, I thought. "Are we going to be in the same cabin?" I asked.

"Probably," he said. "It depends on how many kids sign up and ages and stuff like that, but I have connections. Even if we don't get to stay together," he said, "the cabins are right next to each other. You aren't worried about that are you?"

"No," I lied.

"We'll be together during most of the day and at night the vampires watch over us."

"The what?" I asked.

"The vampires. They aren't real vampires, idiot. That's what we call the night rounds crew. They're counselors who wear headlamps and backpacks full of low treatment and come to the cabins during the night to check our blood sugar and make sure we're okay. They take care of us if we're low, and if we are real low, they take us to Cabin Mufasa."

"To what?" I asked.

"Cabin Mufasa. It's named after the huge, powerful, male lion, Mufasa who is the King of the Pride Lands at the start of the *The Lion King*. He's a wise and fair ruler, who follows the "Circle of Life". Anyway, they give us snacks there and bring our sugar up. Hey, you aren't getting worried about going, are you?"

"No," I said. "I'm fine."

"Wasn't that something at the party?" he said. "I couldn't believe you kissed her like that. I thought her father was going to kill you. I bet he never lets you see her again. It's okay. Wait till you see the girls in camp.

****

Lou Ellen avoided me at school. At lunch she ate with her girl friends. She said it wasn't a good idea for us to hang around together until her father cooled off a little. I figured she would just sneak behind his back and see me and call me anyway. But she didn't, and Mary Jane said it wouldn't be fair if she saw Tony when I couldn't see Lou Ellen (which I knew was Lou Ellen's idea). Tony said he didn't mind because he didn't really like her that much anymore anyway. He said she was too quiet.

When the mail came from the camp a week later, I opened it and read it to myself:

CIRCLE OF LIFE CAMP CONFIRMATION

A space has been reserved for <u>Jimmy James Johnson</u> at Session I of the Circle of Life Camp from July 31 to Aug 5

The camp has received your deposit. Our records show an outstanding balance. This amount must be paid in full and all forms must be completed and returned by June 30 or you will risk losing your reserved spot.

I looked up from the letter and gulped. Two weeks!

Once a completed application is received (all forms and full payment) additional information will be sent regarding camp directions, what to bring, drop-off/pick-up, etc. Tuition is non refundable after July 7.

I looked at the calendar again. *Three* weeks.

Tony's parents started doing better. They got some of their investment money back and didn't lose their jobs, so they decided they didn't have to move and wanted to throw a graduation party for Tony. At first we got excited, thinking we could invite the girls and kids from our class, and then we found out that it was only for Tony and me, my parents and his.

"What would we wear to a dinner party like that?" my mother asked. "I heard that his parents lost a lot of money with their investments, but they are far from poor. I'm sure their idea of a dinner party is different from ours."

V.T. Dacquino

"We'll wear what we usually wear when we go out to dinner," my father said. "How bad can it be? We'll just be ourselves."

CHAPTER 15

Mr. Papalardi stood in front of our graduating class and made his final speech to us:

"And so class, you are now at a special time in your lives. Robert Frost, one of our greatest poets, said that we sometimes stand at a crossroads. We stand at a fork where we must decide whether to take a road that is well-travelled, or take the road less-travelled by. That is where you stand now. Will you do what many others have done before you and what you have always done, or will you view today as your new beginning? Is today the first day of the rest of your life?" He looked right at me, and said, "Will you weigh your differences and let them hold you back, or will they take you down a road that will enable you to be all that you can be?"

Everyone in the audience gave him a huge round of applause and when Lou Ellen and her girlfriends gave him a standing ovation, everyone

109

stood with her. I watched her standing there in her white dress clapping and smiling and I wished I could kiss her again the way I did at her party, but I knew it wasn't going to happen.

Lou Ellen's parents rushed her out of the auditorium right after the ceremony and I knew exactly where she was going. Her parents were throwing a graduation party for her and her *girl*friends.

Tony's parents were standing with mine at the punch bowl. They didn't sit with us during the speeches because they got there late.

"Wasn't it a lovely ceremony?" Tony's mother said. Her long blonde hair was up and she was wearing a real sparkly dress with a diamond necklace; she looked like she was going to some kind of a Hollywood celebration. His father had his moustache and beard trimmed perfectly and he was wearing a dark grey suit with a white shirt and tie. I told Tony how great they looked and he said my parents looked good too, but I know he was just saying that, because they looked just like everyone else's parents. My father was wearing black dress pants, a light blue shirt, and a dark blue sport jacket; my mother was wearing her favorite red and black dress.

Tony rode in the black Town car with his parents and we followed them in ours. When we got to the house, Vinny stopped at the top of the circle and let the three of them out. Then he came to our car and opened the door for my mother and helped her out. My father and I got out by ourselves and joined everyone. We stood there for about five minutes until an older woman in a black dress and apron opened the front door. She motioned for us to come in and we all stood together in the front hall. It wasn't the first time I had seen it; I passed through it a lot of times on my way to Tony's room. I could tell my parents were impressed because they were staring at the murals painted into the walls and at the long winding staircase with the huge chandelier over it. Vinny had to say, "Ahem" to get their attention. He was standing by two huge carved doors that led into the dining room. I had never been in there before and I was amazed; Tony and I always ate in the kitchen or in his bedroom. It sure didn't look anything like our dining room.

His parents were already standing by their chairs at the long table. It was set like one of those real fancy restaurants in New York City with about a million dishes, glasses, lighted candles and bouquets of flowers. The chandeliers were on real dim and the fireplace had a fire in it, which was a little weird because it was pretty warm out.

After we all sat down again, the maid who had come to the front door came in with hot appetizers on a tray and then Vinny came out with champagne and soft drinks for me and Tony. His father raised his glass and said, "Here's to our graduates."

After we toasted, I looked at what I had taken from the maid's tray and it didn't look like anything I wanted to eat. My father was staring at it too. It was brown and mushy in spots with a hard shell on it and was sitting on a cracker. I think mine moved! I hid it under my plate and was praying it didn't crawl out. When my father ate his, I watched the expression on his face and almost died laughing. Tony wasn't looking at me, so I couldn't tell if he had eaten his. His hands were folded on his lap and he was staring down into his plate.

No one really talked about much at dinner; I think they had some kind of rule about not talking at the dinner table. It was pretty weird for me and my parents because that's where we talk to each other the most.

When dinner was over, his parents took their napkins from their laps, put them on the table, and told Tony he was excused. We were both pretty happy about finally being excused to his bedroom. His room doesn't have a fireplace in it like mine, but it's bigger and has a large flat screen TV. He went to turn it on and I said, "Wait a minute." I took a deep breath and tried to get up my courage to tell him my decision about camp. "I need to talk to you about something important."

"Hang on a minute before you tell me. I want to hear what they're saying."

"Who?" I said.

"Our parents," he said. He smiled and opened his closet door then got down on one knee by a little heating vent. He put his ear closer to it and whispered, "Listen."

His mother was saying something. "We cannot thank you enough for allowing the boys to spend so much time together. JJ is a lovely boy."

Tony smiled and pinched my cheek and I slapped his hand away. He laughed quietly and listened again.

"We appreciate your coming here this evening," his mother continued. "Things have been difficult for him since our move here." She paused. "And now that things have been better for him it will all be taken away, ---" She paused a real long time now and Tony practically had his ear to the floor. "I'm afraid we have not been quite honest with Tony about our situation." She paused again and I almost wanted to shout for her to hurry up and finish what she was saying. "We've run into difficulty with our finances and are accepting an offer for the house. I'm afraid that Tony will not be returning to the schools here in the fall. We're hoping the boys can still be together at camp, but he'll be moving in with his grandmother for a while. It hasn't been easy for him there. His

113

cousins are quite cruel to him and tease him incessantly about his diabetes. He had no other friends. Since he also had no friends here, we hired Vinny as his caretaker and friend, but we've had to drastically reduce Vinny's responsibility for him which made us quite thankful for JJ. His grandmother is our only alternative for the summer since we are going to be much too occupied with all of this business at hand to properly supervise him now that school is out. I do wish you could encourage JJ to spend some time with him at camp."

Tony stood up and motioned with his head for me to get out of his closet. I felt real sorry for him. He just put the TV louder and sat there like he was watching it. When the little knock at the door came, I said, "Hey, Tony."

"Don't talk," he said. "I know what you're thinking. I don't need you to be my friend because you feel sorry for me. Just go."

CHAPTER 16

I was furious with Tony. What kind of friend did he think I was? How could he even think I would be like that? I couldn't wait to tell him how I felt; but he didn't come to school on the half day after graduation. He must have sent Vinny or someone to clean out his locker, because it was open and empty when I came out of Mr. Papalardi's class for the last time.

I called his house the next day and the maid said he was at his grandmother's for the summer. I tried to call Lou Ellen a few days after that, but her father answered and I hung up. One of the kids from my class said she was at sleep-away camp with Mary Jane until August. I was bored to death and angry at Tony for not talking to me; I didn't tell my parents that Tony and I had heard what his mother had said. I just knew that I *wasn't* going to go to camp. They never even asked why Tony didn't walk us to the door or car when it was time to leave.

****

I sat on my bed, held up my "final confirmation notice" and read through it. It gave me directions to the camp and arrival and departure dates and explained the "accommodations." It warned me that tuition was now non-refundable and then it said what I had to bring with me:

What to Bring:

Bring clothes appropriate to the weather; include warm clothes for cold nights, and a bathing suit.

I sighed then took a deep breath. At least if I didn't go I wouldn't have to be a "little dipper."

Two pairs of sneakers are recommended and/or hiking boots. Bring a flashlight, extra batteries for the flashlight, insect repellent, extra socks, tooth brush and paste, shampoo, soap, towels, bedding, (either sleeping bag or sheets and blankets) pajamas if you choose, and pillows. Sunscreen is required.

OTHER IMPORTANT INFORMATION

All meals and snacks are provided, as well as reaction treatments (glucose tabs, juice and candy) please do not bring your own candy for reaction treatments. Beverages are provided. PLEASE NOTE THAT THE CAMP WILL PROVIDE THE CAMPERS WITH BLOOD GLUCOSE MONITORS, STRIPS, INSULIN AND SYRINGES. All medication must be kept in the nurse's cabin.

Why couldn't he trust me? I could have told him that I didn't have any friends before I met him. It was no big deal. I could have talked to him. I folded the papers to put them away and prepared myself to break the bad news to my parents, and then, like magic, the phone rang.

"Hello?"

"I'm sorry I wasn't honest with you. I just didn't know what to say. I didn't want you to think I was a loser without friends."

"You are a loser," I said. "I tried to be your friend and you didn't trust me."

"I was wrong," he said, "that's all I've been thinking about while I was up here. Will you still come to camp? I didn't lie to you about that. I

117

really do have friends there and it's a great place. I really miss not having you around and I need to talk to you. Will you come? I know I was a jerk."

"You are a jerk. You should have told me the truth," I said. "We were friends."

"*Were* friends? Does that mean we aren't anymore? You aren't coming?" he asked. He sounded like he was going to cry or something.

Neither one of us said anything for a while, and then I said, "Yes. I'm coming. I miss you, too."

"Really?" he said. "You're really coming? Do you still have all of the papers from the camp? I was just going through my list of things to bring. Did you go over your list yet? Don't worry if you forget anything. They always have enough of everything and you can borrow anything you want from me. Are you really coming? Are we still friends?"

"Yeah," I said. "I'm coming. We'll talk about the friends part."

"We will," he said. "We're in the same cabin!"

"*Really*?" I said.

"Yes, I spoke with the director in case you decided to come. And I promise I'll be honest with you if you ask me about anything. I'll even tell you things about my idiot cousins and my parents."

"You don't have to tell me anything you don't want to," I said.

118

"I know," he said. "I *want* to tell you. I have to hang up now because I'm calling from my grandmother's phone. I can't wait to see you. Bye."

I sat back on my bed and looked through the papers again. "Here goes nothing," I told myself, and then I smiled thinking about Tony.

****

On the day we were scheduled to leave, my mother was worse than I was. Her eyes kept filling with tears and she was starting to make me worry again about going. Finally, my father said, "Enough you two. JJ, you're going to camp. Help put this stuff in the trunk and let's get on the road. We have to be there no later than 6 pm and it's already 3:30. The least bit of traffic is going to get us there late. For goodness sake, he's thirteen," he told my mother. "He isn't a baby."

My mother sighed and said, "Fine." She bent down and grabbed one of my bags and we were on the road. We headed up the Taconic Parkway and kept going toward Albany; I kept the MapQuest directions in my hand the whole way. When we got to Route 90, we counted out the exits and took the side roads to the camp entrance. There was a huge sign in front of us and right at the base of the sign was a hot looking black 1994 Firebird T-top convertible. It was a classic, and it was in mint condition.

Next to it was a crazy maniac waving his hands, shouting, "He's here!"

My mother and father were as happy as I was to see Tony. The second the car stopped I ran over to him and he hugged me. My father walked up to the Firebird and said. "Is this yours?"

Vinny looked proud enough to burst. "Yeah," he said. "Mr. and Mrs. Comabella let me pick up Tony in my own car. They couldn't make it to bring him here. They had a 'few things to tie up.'"

"Nice wheels," my father said. "It looks like it can make some good time."

"Thanks," Vinny said, and then he looked at his watch and said, "You don't have bad timing yourself, sir. It's 5:55. We'd better get them in there."

We drove down the long dirt road to the cabins and parked next to about 40 other cars. Most of the parents and campers were there already. After we got the car unloaded, Tony hugged everyone. It seemed like everybody in there loved him. It made me feel a little left out at first, but Tony introduced me to the people he knew and they started being just as friendly to me; they asked me a million questions.

Tony pointed out the bathrooms and showers; they were covered in paintings and sayings that kids had created. "We call the showers the 'warthog wash.' If you look out this way, you can see Snyder's' Lake and the docks we use for swimming and canoeing." I almost asked him where the "little dippers" swam. "To the right of that is where the medical staff sleeps. To the left of that is where we have our campfires. To the left of that, is the pavilion where we perform our skits." I groaned out loud, and my mother looked at me but didn't say anything. "The nurses are under there today registering the campers," Tony continued. Then he led us across a field that separated two rows of cabins. He pointed to five of them on our left and said, "Those are the girls' cabins and right across from them, on my right, are our cabins."

The cabins were actually little white and green houses with two windows on each side and a door facing the cabin next door. "At the end of the day, we meet right here in the middle with the counselors and hang out under the stars and talk to the girls until the counselors chase us back to our cabins at about 11:00. It's one of the best parts of camp."

"Yeah, I'm sure it is," my father said, and laughed.

Jake, the Director, was waiting for us at a place called Hakuna Matata, a big white building that looked like a chapel. Tony said Jake used to be a camper, then counselor-in-training, then counselor, then director.

"Hakuna Matata?" my father said.

"Yes," Jake said. "It's Swahili. It means 'There are no worries.' A place where there are no problems too big to handle. It's where we do our blood sugar testing and our insulin. Before we go in, though, we need to call your counselor up here to meet you."

When Tony saw who our camp counselor was, he said, "Yes! We got David!" He walked over and shook hands with him and introduced us. "David, meet JJ. He's my best friend from school." He looked at me to see if that was okay to say and I just raised my eyebrow at him, and then smiled.

"Hey, JJ," David said. "Are you ready for some camp fun?"

"I guess so," I said.

"We're going to change that answer to 'absolutely' real quick. C'mon, we need to get your name tag and medical supplies and then we'll go down to the pavilion to meet Nurse Katie. Are these your parents?" My mother and father shook his hand and he told them they needed to tag along with us. He told them to just speak up if they had any questions.

We went into the building and he said, "This is where you'll get your medical supplies and the med box you'll use at camp. The med box isn't decorated yet, but you'll do that while you're here. There are things in the box for you already, such as your meter, your lancing device, lancets, and strips. We'll keep the box locked up for you, but you can take some of the real cool things with you that were donated to the camp from medical companies. They give us freebies like water bottles, laundry bags, camp diaries, and backpacks. We also need to get your bed signs on the table over there. Your bed sign's important for when you pick out your bed. In the middle of the night the vampires need to know who's hiding under the covers."

My parents gave a weird look when he said 'vampires' so I explained what they were. When we were through getting everything from Hakuna Matata, David took my med box, brought it to a nurse at a table to lock up, and stepped away from us for a minute before hurrying back.

"Excellent," he said, Nurse Katie doesn't have a line. We need to hurry down to the pavilion. She needs to register you. She has all of the paperwork you sent here before-hand. She'll want to know that your medical information is all updated. Do you give yourself your own injections?"

"Yes," I said.

"Cool," David said. "You've only been diagnosed for a couple of months, right? He looked at my parents and said, "That's real good. It took me a lot longer than that to be on my own."

"Yes, he's done very well. You have diabetes?" my mother asked.

"Most of us do," he said. "Even Dr. Alicia, the Executive Director and some of the nurses have diabetes. You'll meet Dr. Alicia. She's the one who started the camp. She's a doctor and stays up here with us the whole time we're here."

After the registration, David brought us over to my cabin to pick out my bed. Tony was already standing by the bunk beds and David said, "You guys are going to have to decide which beds you want and who gets top or bottom."

Tony and I answered at exactly the same time. Tony said "top" and I said "bottom." David shook his head and said, "No wonder you guys are best friends." He asked for our bed signs and put them on the beds we picked. I was pretty happy about getting the bottom bunk; I wanted to be sure I could get out of bed quickly if I had to.

We dumped all of my stuff onto my bed and walked back out to the field, "Well, it's almost 7:00." David said. "Everyone starts gathering about now." He looked at my parents and said, "This is the part I hate. I have to get up in front of all of the parents and campers and give a little speech about myself. It's to give parents and new campers a chance to meet all of the counselors and staff." He looked back at me and said, "Your parents will be leaving soon and all the campers and counselors will have a volleyball game. It's girls against the boys. Are you good? I'm the organizer of the volleyball game."

"I'm okay," I said. But I couldn't believe how lucky I felt; the only sport in gym class I ever did great in was volleyball.

The Executive Director, Dr. Alicia, introduced herself and told us more about the camp; at about 7:45, I was walking my parents back to the car. Other kids were in the parking lot with their parents, too. Tony was saying good-bye to Vinny.

"Make sure you follow all the rules," my mother said to me, "and if there are any problems, don't be afraid or embarrassed to call us. Jake said you aren't allowed to use your cell phone while you're here but you can use the camp phone anytime you want. If your blood sugar---"

"Mom," I said. "All of the other parents are leaving." She leaned toward me and I said, "What are you doing? Don't be kissing me in front of everyone."

My father laughed a little, but he didn't say anything.

"Fine," she said. "We'll see you in a few days."

"Fine," I said.

When they finally pulled away and were turning the bend in the road, I felt a little lonely. I still wasn't so sure this was the greatest idea.

125

"Hey, are you going to stand there all day watching them leave?" Tony asked. I turned around and Vinny was backing out of his parking space.

"Take it easy you guys," he said through his open window. "I'll see you in a few days."

Tony turned to me and started to fake cry, "Don't leave me here alone," he said between sobs, and pretended that he was blowing his nose on my shirt. I pushed him away from me and Vinny laughed, waved, and peeled out.

CHAPTER 17

We walked up to the main field and the other kids were gathered there already. A volleyball net was set up and kids were getting into position. David was organizing the boys, and one of the most beautiful girls I've ever seen in my entire life was organizing the girls. She was wearing tennis shorts and a camp tee-shirt.

"Put your eyes back into your head," Tony said. "That's Rose. She's a counselor and she's nineteen."

I didn't answer him. I couldn't keep my eyes off of her. Her long brown hair was down to her shoulders and her build was like one of those girls in a beauty pageant.

Suddenly, I heard "*JJ.*" and jumped at the sound of my name. It was David. "I have you and Tony on the back line at the start of the game. Make sure the ball doesn't get by you. You'll rotate to the front when the time comes. Okay everyone, listen up. This is the first team to play tonight. Before we begin playing, we'll start on the girls' team and each player will shout out her name so we can all get to know each other. When the girls are done giving their names, we'll move to the boys. The next teams for the next two games will do the same. Now before we even do that, the camp Director has a few words for you."

Jake, the Director, came up next to him and cleared his throat like he was about to give some big speech. "Before we get into all the rules and how things go here....can someone tell us what the first rule of camp is?"

A bunch of kids were raising their hands; Jake called out, "Jessica?"

The blond haired girl screamed out, "We are not diabetics!"

Jake laughed and several kids cheered. "Yes," Jake said, "We never refer to ourselves or other people with diabetes as *diabetics*. We are not now and never will be a disease! I have never been "diabetic" I have always been Jake who just happens to have diabetes." I heard a few kids around me talking and saying, "Cool" and "Somebody should tell my school that!"

Jake continued, "Ok, we'd like to welcome you officially now that your parents aren't here. You have all met your counselors and we want to remind you that they are here for you. If you are low, go to your counselor, if you need to go to the bathroom during the night, remember the bathrooms are not in your cabin, but your counselor is. If you have any concerns or questions, go to your counselor. Also, remember another important rule of the camp: respect yourself and each other for not only your similarities to others, but also for your differences."

The kids cheered when he said that, and David said, "Okay, let the games begin!"

Rose was the first girl to give her name and her voice was as beautiful as she was. The other girls gave their names too but all I could hear was Rose. When it was the boys' turn to say our names I said mine loud and clear. And I was glad, too. The first serve came directly to me and I hit it perfectly into our front line where one of our boys spiked it over for a point. Everyone started yelling things like, "Great job, JJ" and "Nice one, JJ"

As the game went on, I only got better, and then the perfect ball came right to me. I spiked it over the net like a pro, but not pro enough. Rose dropped to her knees and sent it straight into the air. A girl next to her stretched up and spiked it back to our side of the net for a point. It was my turn to serve. I took a deep breath, tossed the ball up, and hit it into the net. Bad serve. A few kids groaned and one of the girls took her position to serve. It was perfect. The ball sailed right into the air into our front line and was tapped back over the net to them, then back to us, then back to them, and back to us, and back to them, and then was sent flying right at me. I wasn't really paying attention and lifted my hands to hit it but I was too late; it hit me smack in my face! The next thing I knew, I was on my butt surrounded by people. I wasn't knocked out or anything, just knocked down, and embarrassed. I looked around at a sea of faces, and the closest one to me was Rose's.

I don't know what made me say it, but I said, "Are you an Angel?" Everybody laughed and Rose said, "He's okay," and then smacked me on the top of my head. Everybody laughed again, especially Tony, and we went back to the game and won.

After all the games were done a loud horn was honked and we had to go to Hakunah Matata for our insulin. I walked in and campers were gathering in circles. I wasn't sure of where to go and then I saw "Timon," the name of my cabin, on the floor with a circle of kids around it. Tony introduced me to a couple of the kids he knew and the other two campers in our cabin introduced themselves. David came up behind me and gave me my med box. "It's time to check your sugar," he said.

I looked around and it was pretty weird to see everyone pricking their fingers and checking their sugar at the same time. There were about fifty kids doing it together with thirty staff members doing it with them like it was normal. I checked my sugar and waited while David walked around the circle getting our readings. Mine was 78 and David said, "You're a little low, but you were low before, too, weren't you? We're going down for a snack together in a little while and we'll be having ice cream. We'll let you talk to the nurse about your carb ratio. Are you okay from that fall you took in the volleyball game?" He smiled and tapped me on the head the way Rose did, and then wrote my reading down in his little record book.

After that it got really weird. Kids started injecting in front of each other. I looked over at Tony and he was lifting his shirt to inject into his stomach. He smiled when he saw me watching him. I had never injected in my stomach, only my arms and legs. I almost did my stomach because he and a couple of the other kids were doing it there, but I couldn't do it; I went ahead and injected into my arm.

After our med boxes were collected we went down to the cafeteria, but we had to hurry because it was starting to rain. When we got inside we waited in line to pick out our flavor of ice cream and the director announced that we were going to announce "Firsts."

"Not bad, right?" Tony said. "I love ice cream."

"Me too," I said. "What are 'firsts'? Can we have seconds if we want?"

He laughed. "Firsts means campers who have done something for the first time. Some kids have never injected by themselves before tonight and stuff like that. We get prizes for it. They're just trying to make us feel good about learning new things here."

We took our seats and the director called out certain kids' names; he announced what their "firsts" were, and everyone hooted and hollered for them. They got to go up and pick things out of a box, like squirt guns, and buttons with funny things written on them. I was shocked when I heard *my* name being called.

"And now a 'first' prize for the camper who was the 'first' to use his *head* during a volleyball game and *face* his situation." All the kids laughed at the joke gift and Rose came over and gave me a little volleyball on a key chain, then tapped me on my head again. The kids roared and I know I blushed. She had changed her clothes and was wearing a camp sweatshirt. I couldn't take my eyes off of her. I was so busy watching her, I almost didn't hear Tony say, "Hello, *Earth to JJ?* Congratulations."

****

At about 10:30 pm we were dismissed to our cabins to get ready for bed and I was pretty tired, but I couldn't wait to gather on the field to sit and talk under the stars. Tony kept saying it was the best part of the day, only it was easy to see that it wasn't going to happen any too soon; it was pouring rain.

We organized our stuff and turned down our beds, and then I slipped on my pajamas and got ready to wash up and brush my teeth. I turned to Tony and it suddenly dawned on me, "Hey," I said, "do we have to go out into the rain to the bathrooms to brush our teeth and get washed for bed?"

"Duh, yeah," he said. "There's no bathroom in here."

I was in my pajamas! I looked around at the other guys and saw that they were wearing sweatpants and tee shirts. I got out of my pajamas real quick and put on my sweats. When I was dressed and everyone was settled down, David announced that we were going to the bathrooms and then would have to check our sugar. He said if we were below 120, we would have to go to Cabin Mufasa for low treatment. We could stay up and talk for as long as we wanted after we returned from the bathrooms if we were not low, otherwise, no one was leaving the cabin to talk to the girls or go anywhere because of the weather. He also told us to check our bed signs so that the vampires could see them during the night when they came around to check our sugar.

Fortunately, David had plastic rain parkas for us and we slipped them on and stood in the doorway. The rain was coming down in bullets. "Are you ready?" David asked. "Go."

We slipped and slid our way across the field and it was amazing fun. I fell twice and had mud all over me. By the time I got to the bathroom, I was soaked and laughing like crazy. Some of the kids took hot showers, but some of the kids, like me and Tony, just washed up at the sink and brushed our teeth.

The trip back to the cabin was even more fun than the trip there. I got to my bed dripping and saw the other kids sliding out of their sweat suits and getting into their pajamas. It was still raining pretty hard when Tony said, "I can't believe this rain. That was fun wasn't it?"

"Yeah," I said, but I was thinking about my sugar. David was calling for us to check it. I was hoping that I wasn't real low and would have to go to Cabin Mufasa; I didn't feel up to running out into the rain again. It was fun but I was pretty tired and ready to rest awhile. I was relieved when the meter read 150.

"What was yours?" Tony asked from his bed.

"150," I said.

"Great," he answered. "Mine's 200. C'mon up."

"What?" I asked.

"C'mon up. We can talk on my bed for a while. You aren't going to sleep right away are you?"

"No," I said, and climbed up with him.

"What do you think? Do you like it so far?" he asked.

"It's good," I said, but I was thinking it was pretty early to tell. It all still seemed strange and I was wondering what my parents were doing at home without me there. I figured they had gone to dinner and were watching some late night movie or something.

"You were pretty funny with Rose today," he said. "The kids really like you. You aren't half bad at volleyball either. We're probably going to play again tomorrow, but we have a lot of other stuff we're going to do first." He stopped talking and sat there trying not to look at me for a minute.

"Listen," I said. "You don't have to say---"

"I know," he said. He looked around again and watched some of the other kids who were having some kind of wastepaper-basketball competition. Are you sorry you came?" he asked.

"What?" I said. "No. I'm having a good time. It's just strange. I don't sleep away from home very much." I was kind of sorry I said it because I was afraid he would think I was homesick or something.

V.T. Dacquino

"I'm used to sleeping away from home," he said. "My parents love getting rid of me. I wish I had real parents like yours. My parents can't wait for summer so they can send me to my grandparents or camp. I hate going to my grandparents' house. I mean, I love them, but the kids up there aren't like you. And it's not just because you have diabetes like me. I don't think you'd be mean to kids with diabetes even if you didn't have it. Those guys up there are just mean to me because I'm not like them. First of all, they hate me because my parents are a lot richer than theirs. They don't know how much I wish we were poor like them so my parents would have time for me. My cousins and their friends say all kinds of mean things and run away when I come into the room; they pretend they're afraid of catching my diabetes. It's like a game for them, but not for me. I think deep inside they really are afraid because diabetes is something they don't understand. Having diabetes isn't half as bad as having their problem."

A bright flash of lightening came right then followed by the loudest rumble of thunder I've ever heard. And then the rain sounded like it was going to come right through the roof. It was the kind of rain that I think I will always remember.

"Did you ever talk to your parents about it? Do they know how you feel?" I asked. He looked at me like I was losing my mind or something.

"I think they wish I was never born; they probably would have loved to have a normal kid they didn't have to worry about instead of having a kid with diabetes like me. I talk to Vinny about it. We talked all the way up here and he said he was going to tell my parents how I felt. I made him promise he would never do that; they would fire him for good if he tried to talk to them about me." He looked at me again, and said, "Do you talk to your father about your diabetes?"

"No," I said.

"You should. He understands us. Don't you wish all people could understand how it feels for kids with diabetes?" I sat there looking at him. I almost wanted to tell him how I thought my father had put a curse on me by writing his book, but I didn't. "I don't know," I said, finally. "But I think you're right about the kids who are mean to you; I would rather have our problem than theirs."

"Me too," he said. "Until I met you, the only other kids I've known with diabetes were the kids in this camp, except for the kids in your father's book. I really liked the kids in his book and the way Jimmy James learned to accept himself. His book helped me to not feel like some kind of freak or something. I don't think I would have been brave enough to come here if I hadn't read his book first. It's real weird that the son of the guy who wrote the book would end up being my best friend.

137

Do you know that you and Mr. Papalardi and the school nurse were the only ones at school I ever told about my diabetes? I was real scared that you wouldn't want to be friends with me. I'm glad we made friends, and I'm sorry I wasn't honest with you. I hope you like it here. I'm tired now and I need to go to sleep. Can you go to your own bed now?"

I wasn't sure if he was kidding until he crawled under the covers and put his head on his pillow. I jumped down and crawled under my own covers. Some of the other kids were still awake and I could hear them talking and playing for a while. Then there was silence and I wished I was home in my own bed. I couldn't sleep. I was thinking about my father and how I had blamed him for my diabetes, and how my parents were always around when I needed them. I lay there thinking and thinking and thinking and listening; above me I could hear Tony's loud snoring. He was making the same kind of sleeping pig noises my father makes when he snores. It made me miss home even more, and then the cabin door creaked open. I held my breath and watched quietly. Two figures came through the door wearing elastic bands around their heads with little lights on them and full length raincoats. In the dark they looked like hunched back monsters with one eye and shiny black skin.

One of them pointed to the right then came to the left on my side of the room. He reached for my hand to wake me up but I said, "Hello."

He jumped up so quickly he hit his head on the bottom of Tony's bunk and gave a little yelp. "Oh, shoot," he whispered. "Don't talk. You'll wake the others."

I could see him a little better now. He was about twenty-five years old and was one of the vampires. "I need to check your sugar," he whispered. "To be sure you aren't too low." He handed me his lancet and meter and I did a finger stick. When the meter beeped and read 90, he wrote it on his clip board and showed it to me. He gave me a thumbs up and reached into his bag for a Chuckles candy, then put his finger to his mouth to tell me to eat it quietly and go back to sleep.

He reached up and woke Tony softly and checked his sugar; the vampire wasn't with him very long and there was no noise or movement after he left. I figured Tony's blood count was high enough that he didn't need extra sugar.

When the vampires left the cabin, I lay there awake. I could barely make out their voices on the two-way radio when they were out by the cabin next door; they were radioing in our readings to the nurse. I listened until the voices faded away completely, and then I started thinking about an idea that I wanted to share with my father; it was

139

an idea that I knew was going to make him real happy.

CHAPTER 18

At 8:30 in the morning, I thought I heard my mother calling me. I jumped up and listened again. "Rise and shine. Good morning," a voice said. It was one of the cooks. She was knocking at our door and shouting loud enough to wake up campers across Snyder's Lake. "First horn is about to go off. Everybody up and at'em."

"We're first horn," Tony's groggy voice said from above me. "We have to get dressed and go to Hakuna Matata to test our sugar and get our insulin. Can you go for me? I'm too tired."

"I can't," I said. "I was out all night sucking blood with the vampires."

He jumped up and poked his head over the side of the bed. "Did you go to Cabin Mufasa last night?" he asked.

"No," I said, "but I did stay awake all night because of someone's snoring."

"Don't be telling me I snore," he said. "I know I don't snore."

"You snore worse than my father," I said.

The rest of the guys were awake and listening from their beds and a kid named Tom said, "That was *you* Tony? I thought real vampires got in here or something."

We all laughed and Tony seemed pretty happy to be getting all the attention. "I think you were all having nightmares at the same time," he said. "I definitely don't snore."

"Yeah, right," another kid said. "Maybe it was the warthog they named the warthog wash after."

We probably would have gone on for a while more but the first horn went off and we had to get dressed and get up to Hakuna Matata. We gathered in circles the way we did the night before and tested our sugar. The camp director told us we'd be having French toast sticks, scrambled eggs, links of sausage, fruit and orange juice. I couldn't believe they had that kind of food there and it would be all right for me to eat all that. My mother always made me only take enough insulin for 75 carbs; I knew that wouldn't be enough this morning because I was starving. When I discussed that with Nurse Katie she told me I could take half my insulin now and half after I eat to account for the extra carbs. Tony laughed when I told him I was starving and having a big breakfast. "I always eat a big breakfast

142

when I'm here," he said, "this place gives me an outrageous appetite."

After our injections we went to the warthog wash and got cleaned up and dressed and waited for the second horn people to join us at breakfast. I couldn't believe how good it was. When we were done, we sat and talked with the kids from our cabin and they started talking about the dance we were going to have.

"I know who JJ's going to ask to dance with him," Tom said.

"Yeah, Rose," Ramos, the other kid, said. They laughed and Ramos said, "I've been thinking about who I'm going to dance with. How about you, Tony?"

Tony said, "Hmmm." He looked around the cafeteria very slowly, and then he said, "That one." Everybody jumped up to get a better look, and I had to admit, she was pretty cute. She had blonde pigtails.

"Okay," Tom said. "I'm picking one out for me." He looked from table to table and finally, he said, "That one with the purple hair."

"Her hair is definitely purple," Tony told him. "And she's new. I hope she can dance."

All the while they were looking for their girls to dance with, I was looking too, but they all seemed a lot older than me. It was real hard to find a girl my own age because *Session I* was for thirteen

143

through sixteen year olds. I almost gave up and then Jake called for our attention and announced the campers who achieved "firsts." He called a girl with short light-brown hair and a cute smile. She got a "first" for injecting in her stomach for the first time. Her name was Chrissie; she was about my age and very good looking.

"Hey," Tony said, "I don't even have to ask who JJ's thinking about dancing with. I haven't seen his eyes pop out so far since he saw Rose walk across the volleyball court. He put his hand on my shoulder and said, "Good choice. That's Christine. We call her Chrissie; she was new last year and she is definitely not only cute but the absolute best dancer in camp."

Great, I thought. Just what I needed, a great dancer whose feet I could step on!

The talking went from the dance to swimming and I was pretty nervous about how excited Tony was getting. "I'm going to spend the whole afternoon swimming," he said. "I've been waiting all winter to jump around on that new trampoline and dive off the far dock."

"It's not a trampoline," Tom said. "It's more like a big inflated raft with a ladder attached."

"Whatever," Tony said. "I only know I can't wait to go on it."

The other kids all agreed with him and I sat there thinking about how I could get out of going there with him. I thought maybe I could pretend I was sick, but I was worried about everyone's reactions. Around here the staff jumped when someone said they were sick.

"Hey, JJ," Tony said. "Are you feeling okay?"

"I think I just ate too much," I said.

At the sound of the horn we finished clearing our tables and gathered outside. Tony thought we were going to have another volleyball game, but it turned out to be kickball. I was pretty glad because anybody knows how to play kickball. I kept my eye on Chrissie hoping she would end up on my team; Tony did but Chrissie didn't. Tony volunteered to pitch and he was really good. He struck out about ten players, including Chrissie. I played way out in the outfield where there really wasn't much action. I was too worried about swimming to enjoy playing. The game was okay; I kicked a good one toward third when we got our ups and made it to first base, but the next kicker scored our third out. I was kind of glad when a snack break was called. Most campers sat around on the ground to eat and Chrissie sat alone under a tree. Tony started to walk over to me but when he saw where I was heading, he stopped and smiled.

"Hi," I said. "Congratulations on your 'first.'"

She looked up at me and smiled back. It was an amazing smile and I couldn't believe how green her eyes were. They looked like the nurse's eyes in *triage* at the children's hospital, only they were greener, and younger, and prettier.

"Thanks. I never thought I would get the nerve to inject into my stomach. Do you inject there?"

"No," I said. "But I'm working on it."

"Well, congratulations on *your* 'first' yesterday, too," she said. She put her hand to her mouth and giggled and it was a real cute kind of giggle.

"Hey, you two," David said from behind us. "The break is over and we're getting the game started again. Come on over with the rest of us."

"Will you be going to the dance tonight?" I asked.

"Everyone goes to the dance, silly," she said. "Do you know how to dance?"

"A little," I said. "You can teach me," I told her. "My name is JJ."

"I know what your name is," she said. She giggled again and I was wishing we were playing Truth or Dare instead of kickball.

After the game we went up to Hakuna Matata for testing and insulin and I couldn't see Chrissie very well; her cabin's circle was all the way on the other side of the building. When I got down to the cafeteria she was at her own table and David said we had to sit together with ours. Tony asked me if I got to talk with her at all and he slapped me five when I said yes.

"I did pretty well too," he said. "The girl with the blonde pigtails is fourteen and she said she doesn't mind that I'm thirteen. She said she'd talk with me at the dance anyway. She has a great accent. How old is Chrissie?"

"I don't know," I said. "I didn't talk to her very long."

"Well, she's cute," he said. "And she's a good dancer. I would offer you lessons but I saw you dancing at Lou Ellen's party. You'll be fine. I can't wait to go swimming after lunch. They're going to give us a test to see how well we can swim and when we pass the test we can go off and jump on the new water trampoline and dive off the far dock."

"Test?" I said.

"Yeah, they won't let us swim in the 'big dippers' area until we prove we can swim well. Can you swim real well?"

I looked at him without talking and shook my head no; he stared back at me, then he started cracking up laughing.

I felt myself getting real angry. "Don't laugh at me," I said.

"I wasn't laughing *at* you," he said. "I was laughing *with* you. Everyone is going to think you're faking it, since the counselor in charge of the little dippers is Rose!"

****

After lunch we went back to our cabins and slipped into our bathing suits. I was pretty nervous about going down to the lake front and not being a good swimmer and finally decided to hold back in the cabin for a few minutes and talk to David about it.

"It's no big deal," he said. "Tony already talked to me and we have it under control. You sure you aren't doing this just to work with Rose or get attention and laughs from the other kids? What happened in the volleyball game was funny, but we take swimming very seriously here. Can you swim or can't you?"

"I don't think I'm good enough to pass the test," I said.

"Okay. You can avoid swimming altogether if you want, but she's a real good instructor and can give you some great tips on swimming. Why don't you give her a shot at helping you? I'll tell her you're serious about working with her. Tony is going to give up his swim time to help you swim better."

Tony was waiting for me outside the cabin and I said, "I don't want you doing it."

"You don't want me doing what?" he asked

"Giving up your swim time for me. You said yourself that you've been waiting all winter for this."

"Listen," he said. "I wasn't a great swimmer when I first started going here either. Rose helped me out, too." He wasn't smiling. He was looking at me straight in the eye like he really wanted me to know he was serious. I kept talking and telling him that I wanted him to go with the other kids, but he just stood there with the same look on his face. When I finally stopped talking, he said, "Are you done? Let's go see Rose and get started."

The lifeguard gathered the other kids by the water's edge and talked to them about the test they had to take to prove that they could swim. I searched the group for Chrissie but she wasn't there. I felt pretty relieved.

"There's nothing to be embarrassed about if you don't pass the test and can't swim well," the lifeguard was saying. "We all know here at camp that no one is perfect. The most important thing is that you're safe and you're having a good time. Now let's get started."

He started calling out names and Tony and I walked to Rose. She was standing by the shallow part of the lake and it was pretty embarrassing since no one else was with her besides me and Tony. Rose said that lake safety wasn't something to take lightly, and she wouldn't tolerate it if we were not being serious about needing help and wanting to learn.

"I don't swim much," I said. "This is the first time I ever went to a sleep over camp where I had to swim; my family doesn't have a pool or go to the beach very often. Tony's only here to help me. He can swim."

She slapped him five and said, "You're darn right he can swim; I taught him." She smiled at him and said, "Okay, that's fine," she said. "Let's see what you can do."

She watched me swim to the dock and back and she told me to keep my head down more and straighten my legs and then asked Tony to demonstrate what she was talking about. Before long I couldn't believe I was actually swimming and passed the test.

"You'll get better as time goes on," she said. "Tony wasn't as good as you when he started here and look at him now. I want you to stay in this area for a little while longer and keep practicing, but after snack you can go on the trampoline with the other campers. We swim in life jackets on the trampoline anyway; just stay with Tony." She looked at Tony and said, "Have you got him covered?"

"Definitely," he said.

"Don't get nervous,' she said. "We have a lifeguard on the trampoline."

We had snack right on the lake front and then went to the trampoline. It was outrageous fun and just as I was getting into it and feeling comfortable in the water, Tony said, "Okay we have to go back and learn a few more strokes. I want you to be confident for canoeing tomorrow."

"Canoeing?" I asked.

He smiled and pointed to a rack of canoes. I took a deep breath and groaned. He laughed and said, "Relax. There's nothing to fear. I've got you covered."

We walked up to the cabin after swim activity and David was waiting there to talk to all of us. "All right, you guys. It's time to start thinking about tomorrow night."

"We didn't even get through tonight yet," Tom said. "Tonight's the dance."

"The dance will take care of itself. Tomorrow night is skit night and every cabin participates, including ours, and that takes preparation. The first thing we have to do is decide what we are going to do. Guys like Tony who have been around a while can give you ideas of what the skits are like, but you can be as creative as you want. Don't worry if it's silly, most of them are. We have plenty of stuff you can use, like costumes, fake instruments and stuff like that. Use your imagination and talk about it on your free time together, which you know by now, isn't very much time. You can talk about it right now for a little while, but you need to get to Group and then get ready for dinner; after dinner you'll have a little more time before you get ready for the dance. You don't need to dress up all that special for the dance, but it would be nice if you clean up a bit and maybe take a shower. Any questions? Any ideas for us Tony?"

"Actually, I do," he said. "Grab a seat and listen up. This idea is real funny."

CHAPTER 19

I tested a little low at supper and so did the rest of my cabin; it was because of all the exercise we were doing. "Your swimming is coming along pretty well," he said. "I was watching you with Rose and Tony. I see a big improvement already. Nice job." He looked over at Tony and said, "How's that skit idea? Did you talk to them about it?"

"Tonight after dinner," he said. And you should stay at our table after you eat, because *you* are in the skit."

"Oh, great," David said. "I can't wait to hear what you have in store for me. And don't forget that we have Group discussions with the staff for about an hour after dinner."

After dinner, Tony had us huddled around the table and was talking real quiet. "Can you all hear me?" Everybody said yeah and he continued. "We're going to be vampires doing night rounds,

153

only we're going to turn out to be real vampires who switched places with the counselors." He looked at David. "You're going to be the night rounds vampire."

Everybody laughed and really seemed to like Tony's idea, but David said, "Don't be thinking I'm going to let any one of you bite my neck."

We all laughed and Tony said, "Nah, I've got that covered. We're going to put our hand on the person's neck and suck on our own hand. It'll just look like we're real vampires."

"Will we get to dress up like vampires?" Ramos asked.

"Of course we will," Tony said. "That's half the fun."

David nodded approvingly. "It sounds like it could work. We'll talk about it again tonight before bed. For now, you need to get ready for discussion groups. We do this by age, so Tom you and Lewis will go together with Ramos and Arnie and meet with the fifteen year olds; JJ and Tony will go with the thirteen and fourteen year olds. After discussions we'll meet back here to finish getting ready for the dance. For those of you who have never been to camp before, Group is where you can talk about your experiences with diabetes. You shouldn't be uptight or embarrassed or shy at Group. You'll be surprised what you can learn.

Remember a lot of us here at camp have gone through a lot of things you are going through."

As soon as we were cleaned up, Tony and I walked across the field toward the cafeteria. Chairs were set up in a circle on the porch and an older guy was sitting on the railing in a camp tee-shirt waiting for us. I had this weird feeling when I saw him; it was like I knew him, but I didn't.

"Look at him a little closer," Tony said. "And try to picture him with a little light on his forehead. That's what vampires look like in the daytime."

There were five of us in the group: three boys and two girls. The vampire introduced himself as Ronnie and said that he was going to lead us in a discussion about diabetes. He said that Group was a good place to talk about what it's like to have diabetes. He said we could talk about that certain teacher, or parent, or doctor who doesn't seem to understand what it's like to be us, or how weird it feels to eat snack in class when no one else is eating anything.

One of the girls introduced herself as Amelia and did a lot of talking. She talked about her father and said that she didn't think her father understood her. "I'm on the school swim team and when I come home from a meet, my father *never* says 'How did you do? Did you win?' he just says, 'Are you feeling okay? Did you test your sugar? Do you need to eat something?' That's all he thinks about."

The group understood her completely and I looked over at Tony to see if he was going to say anything, but he didn't. I wanted to know more about his cousins and parents and stuff, but he just nodded and agreed with most of what the other kids said. When Ronnie asked him how things were for him, he just said, "They're okay."

When Ronnie asked me how I was doing, I said, "I haven't been diagnosed very long. Is it okay if I just listen to what some of the other kids say?"

"Sure," Ronnie said. "We don't force anyone to talk about themselves here, but it's always good to share your feelings. It's nice to find out that you aren't alone."

Amelia and the other boy made up for me and Tony not talking much and I was pretty glad. I didn't think I was ready to talk about my father.

****

The camp hired an older guy from town to be the DJ and he had his own decorations and CD's. I was afraid he was going to have music that was from my parents' dances, but he had a pretty cool collection. He also had a colored glass ball that he hung from the pavilion and it made a million colorful floating circles when a light was shined into it. The picnic tables were all pushed to one side of the concrete floor and there was a table with

156

a cooler of Crystal Light and cold water. The cups were set up in some kind of pyramid. All of the lights were off except for the ball and as it got dark out, the dots kept circling the dance floor. I almost couldn't see the girls on their side of the pavilion.

I was wearing my best jeans and my best tee shirt that I was saving for the dance; I had my hair combed back the best I could. I used gel to make it stay back and not dangle over onto my forehead. Tony was wearing his jeans and last year's camp shirt, but his hair was too short to comb back. The girls took a lot more time trying to look good than the boys.

Chrissie had on white pants and a yellow top and she had matching beads around her neck and hair. I could see that she must have made them in the art room. The music was playing already and I walked toward her.

"Good luck," Tony said.

"Yeah, you too," I said, but I couldn't see the girl with the blonde pig tails anywhere. When I got to Chrissie, she said, "I like your hair combed back like that," and smiled her great smile.

"I like your beads," I said.

"Thank you. I made them in the craft room this afternoon while you were swimming with Rose. The window of the craft room overlooks the lake."

157

I felt real embarrassed and knew I was red. "She was teaching me how to swim," I said. "I'm not very good at it."

She put her hand to her mouth the way she does and giggled. "Sure, I bet," she said. "I saw you swimming. You didn't look that bad at swimming to me. I bet you know how to dance, too."

"I really don't," I said. "I just try to move to the music."

Just as she said that a new song came on. It was a Hannah Montana song.

"Okay, let's see you dance," she said.

I turned around and gulped. No one was on the dance floor.

"No one's dancing yet," I said. "Everyone will be watching us."

"So?" she said. "Dance."

I listened to the beat and tried to get my hips and feet to go along with the rhythm but I couldn't get my body parts to work together. She was *real* good, but suddenly she stopped dancing.

"Well what do you know," she said. "You were telling the truth. You really *can't* dance." She giggled her giggle and I was pretty embarrassed about my dancing.

"Let's go get some Crystal Light," she said.

We walked over to the drinks table and Tony was there with the girl with the blonde pigtails--- only she wasn't wearing pigtails. Her hair was combed straight and she looked a whole lot better than she even did this afternoon.

"JJ, meet PJ," Tony said.

"PJ?" I asked

"JJ?" she asked

"It's short for Patty Jean," she said. I was listening to her but I couldn't believe what I was hearing. She had a real heavy English accent.

"Mine's short for Jimmy James," I said, and smiled at her.

"You aren't going to believe this," Chrissie said, "But I'm here too." She looked at me and said, "Remember me?"

"I remember you," Tony said.

"Oh, this is Chrissie. Chrissie meet PJ," I said.

"Nice to meet you," Chrissie told her. Then she turned to Tony, "I can't believe you aren't dancing. Last year you danced practically every dance."

Tony looked a little embarrassed and said, "PJ isn't big on dancing."

"Wow, neither is JJ," Chrissie said. "Would you two mind if Tony and I danced?" PJ and I looked at each other and it was like some kind of magic connection. We both said "That's okay" at the same time, only hers was in her English accent and I loved listening to it.

Tony and Chrissie danced about 20 dances in a row and I was real happy about it. PJ practically talked my ear off; she talked about England and coming here two years ago and how it was when she got diagnosed and how much she loved living Upstate. I told her about Tony's cousins and their friends and she said that kids where she lives aren't anything like that. She said that kids Upstate were sensitive and made great friends, and the way Tony's cousins acted had nothing to with where they lived. She said ignorant people could live anywhere, even in England. It was like so amazing; the more she talked the more I liked her.

Before I knew it, the DJ was asking if everyone had a good time and he hoped he could come back next year. He said some other things too, but I couldn't really hear him since PJ was still talking and I didn't want to miss anything she was saying.

"Here they come now," she said.

"What?" I asked.

"Tony and Chrissie," she said. "They're done dancing."

"Hey, I can't believe you two never left this spot," Tony told us. "I hope you don't mind that Chrissie and I kept dancing."

"No," PJ said, "I didn't mind at all." Only it didn't sound like she said "at all." It sounded like "atole." I loved that accent.

Chrissie just shrugged and told Tony she wanted a Crystal Light and after he got it for her, Tony said, "We have to gather up at the cafeteria for snack. After that the four us can sit on the field and talk for a while until they force us to go to bed. What do you think?"

"That would be great," PJ said, and she looked right at me when she said it.

****

We talked and laughed and it was the greatest feeling ever to be sitting out there with new friends on the lawn at night. PJ looked up into the stars and said, "I can't believe they are the same stars my family might be looking at right now in England."

Chrissie said, "You aren't going to start singing that song 'Somewhere Out There' from the Walt Disney movie are you?"

We all laughed a little and PJ said, "No, I'm afraid I can't dance nor sing. I spend most of my time writing." We all kind of looked at her surprised.

"JJ's father's a writer," Tony said. I wanted to kick him and changed the subject.

"What do you write?" I asked.

"Poetry mostly," she said.

"That's pretty cool," Chrissie said. "Can you recite one of your poems?"

"I'm afraid my poems aren't very cheerful," she said.

"Can we hear it anyway?" I asked.

"Yeah," Tony said, "Let us hear one."

V.T. Dacquino

"Okay," she said. She adjusted herself on the grass and looked at us one at a time as she recited her poem:

We can all be proud of children
Made of gold or finest silver
For no matter how we rub them
They get shinier each day

But what shall we do for children
Made of delicate fine crystal
Who no matter how we touch them
May get shattered anyway

No one said a word. We all just looked at her. I think maybe Chrissie and Tony were thinking about what the poem meant to them the way I was, because Chrissie said, "I'm not just saying this, PJ. I love that poem. It's exactly what I feel like sometimes. I think, why couldn't I be like other kids who don't have anything wrong with them."

Tony said, "I think it means that maybe some people are afraid to love people with diabetes because they think something is going to happen to them."

No one talked again, until Tony said, "I think we should go back to our cabins now."

The other campers stayed out for a little while longer until the counselors made them go in to bed.

David checked everyone's sugar as they came in and no one said anything about rehearsing or talking about the skit. Tony was real quiet and just lay there up in his bed thinking. I know he was thinking about his parents and what the poem meant. He was thinking the same way I was: Were we "gold or finest silver" who were going to shine no matter what was happening to us? Or were we going to just get shattered like "the delicate fine crystal" in his parents' chandeliers?

CHAPTER 20

Ronnie came and tested me during the night, but I didn't say anything to him and he didn't talk to me. He just tested my sugar and gave me the "thumbs-up" when he checked my reading; I stayed up thinking for a little while and fell back to sleep. The next thing I knew, I heard the cook shouting, "Rise and shine. Good morning."

We got up and got ourselves ready and everything was pretty much like yesterday until Tony sat up and said, "We have to talk about our skit before we go up to Hakuna Matata."

No one complained. We just listened as he talked about how we would paint our faces white and wear black capes and run around like we were flying over the camp looking for our victims and get chased out by the camp vampires who were doing their rounds.

"That's cool," Ramos said. "The real vampires could say something like 'Who are you?' And the camp vampires could say, 'We work here. Go find your own camp.' And the real vampires would say 'Can't we just share?" And the camp vampires would say, "No, they're our campers. Go find your own campers somewhere else.' And the real vampires would say, "Geez. Okay, fine, if that's how you want to be about it, but can we have one of those great little lights on your head? They would be great for seeing in the dark.' And the camp vampires would say, "Okay fine, but don't ever come here again.' And the real vampires would say, 'Okay,' and fly away into the night."

We all looked at him amazed until Tony said, "I suppose that can work. Let's get up to Hakuna Matata and we'll talk about it later."

We gathered in our circles and I looked for PJ. She was there in her blonde pigtails again and I walked right up to her. "I'm sorry if my poem bothered everyone," she said. "I hope you aren't mad at me."

"No," I said. "It's a real good poem. It would only bother me if I weren't gold or silver. No matter how you rub me I get shinier each day."

She smiled a huge smile and was going to say something but Tony was standing behind us and he said, "You'd better not rub him here, the Director will get angry."

PJ got real red and then we all laughed and went to our circles. Before she went, PJ said, "Will I see you later, JJ?"

"Of course," I said.

David brought us our med boxes and I looked into mine for a minute before I prepared my syringe with half my insulin the way Jake taught me so I could have a big breakfast, then I lifted my shirt. Tony watched me take a deep breath and inject into my stomach. "Did you ever inject into your stomach before?" he asked from across the circle.

"Nope," I said. He smiled and gave me thumbs up.

I ate a real good breakfast and when it was over, Jake called up the campers who had achieved "firsts." When I went for mine, Chrissie shouted out, "Yeah, JJ!" I felt real good about myself.

And when Tony's name got called, he was totally surprised, and so was I. Jake said, "And this next 'first' goes to a camper who put himself second and gave up what he wanted to do to put his friend first."

When he called Tony up, Rose gave him a pack of sugarless cherry *Life Savers* and tapped him on the head the way she did to me. The crowd went wild with whoops and hollers; Tony was proud enough to burst.

We spent the rest of the morning playing a game called Alien Encounter. Cones are placed all over the camp with questions under them. Some of the questions were called pop-culture or sports questions like, "Who won last year's World Series?" or "Who was the reigning King of Pop until a tragedy in 2009?" There were also a lot of diabetes questions, like, "What are the seven common injection sites?" The goal is to run around the camp with your cabin and be first to get all of the questions answered. One member of the group records the answers to the questions. When campers are at a cone they are "safe," but between each cone they could be attacked by the camp staff who are dressed as "Aliens" in real weird outfits like hula skirts and adult feet pajamas. If an "Alien" gets you, he can "tag" you with a sock filled with flour and baking powder. If you get "marked" you and the kids in your cabin have to sit down "frozen" until you are forced to do an activity like having to play a baby game like "Duck, Duck, Goose" or "Leap Frog." Once you play the game, you can continue to look for your questions and try to be the first cabin to get done. I got pretty tired playing, but it was definitely fun.

Canoeing was awesome and I got to be with Tony, Chrissie, and PJ in one canoe; it was great how it worked out. We were with David and another counselor and went all over Snyder's Lake.

Everything was so beautiful around the lake and I loved being that close to the people I wanted to be with. Tony must have felt the same way because he asked PJ if she could write a poem about the experience; she said she thought we had enough of her poetry for one weekend.

After dinner, Tony got the cabin together to rehearse the skit. We all agreed that we should use Ramos' idea and we added a lot to it but it was the same basic idea, and funny. We practiced dressing up as real vampires and even got David to dress up as a camp vampire. It was so funny; we made him pretend that every time he gave a camper a low-treatment, he would say, "one for you and one for me" and we had him tuck clothes under his shirt like he was real fat.

Chrissie's cabin did a show based on the old Broadway play *West Side Story* and it was good. Chrissie played Maria and one of the girls in her cabin was dressed as a boy and played Tony. She wasn't anything like *our* Tony.

My favorite was PJ. She did lip sync from a Hannah Montana album with the girls from her cabin and they were awesome. She looked so great that it didn't matter what she did up there and when she introduced the act, everyone was listening to her because of her accent. Our act was the sensation of the night. It made absolutely no sense by the time we actually played it out, but everyone was laughing so hard they made all of *us* laugh and then they just laughed harder. It was a riot.

We had snack after the show and Jake told us to take it easy on the eating because we were going to roast marshmallows at the camp fire. Chrissie, PJ, Tony, and I tried to sit way in the back at the campfire by ourselves, but David said, "I don't think so," and made us sit up front. They gave us some song sheets and led us in all kinds of singing and it was one of those things that becomes a kind of photo album in your mind.

When the camp fire was over, the Director said it was too late to sit out in the field, but we did anyway for a little while and David was worse than my mother at nagging us to go in. When we said our final good-bye, PJ said, "Please don't ever forget me," and kissed me on the cheek. I was thinking, "I couldn't if I tried." And reached over and kissed her on the lips.

David said, "Now! JJ. Good night PJ."

She giggled and said, "Good night, David."

At the end of the night I lay there waiting for the camp vampires thinking about PJ and Tony and everything that went on at the camp. I hated that this was the last night instead of the first, but it made my idea for my father even more important than ever.

I woke up to the sounds of the cook again and was still a little sad about having my parents come to pick me up. I was wishing that 4:30 would never come. And then it did. Cars started pulling up to the parking area and when I saw my parents pull up, my stomach felt sick. PJ's parents came and it was weird to hear them all talking in the same accent. They said it was real great to meet me and I introduced her to my parents. They said they wanted to sit together at the final ceremony. Tony was standing off to the side with David and Tom from our cabin and the real shocker came when the black Lincoln Town Car pulled up to the parking lot. I looked at Tony and he had a weird expression on his face. He was thinking what I was thinking: Why didn't Vinny bring his own car? I think it made him nervous, because he signaled with his head for me to come with him. When the tinted window was lowered, we saw that it wasn't Vinny at all. Tony's parents had come to get him.

CHAPTER 21

On August 31, a few days before school was going to start, it was my father's birthday; I held his present on my lap. In my hand was the poem that PJ had given me before we left each other:

Sometimes something special happens
And it becomes perfectly clear
That we have just changed
We begin the first day of the rest of our lives
Knowing that we have been given
A treasure of gold and silver
That will shine for us forever

Please call me. My number is: 555-424-5544--- love, PJ

I read the poem again to myself and smiled as I thought about the look on Tony's face when his parents got out of the car and hugged him.

"Vinny had a long talk with us on Friday," his father said. "I don't know how we could have been so blind," he hugged Tony and I could see that Tony was fighting back tears.

"We sold the house," his mother said. "And bought a smaller one in the neighborhood. We promise we will try to be there for you in the future."

Tony started crying like crazy right about then and his father said, "Big boys don't cry."

I was thinking, if big boys don't cry, why was I doing it?

****

My mother called me into our dining room and said that we were ready to sing Happy Birthday to my father. I took my present in my hand and went in with them. We sang and I handed him his gift. He raised his eyebrows and opened the gift slowly.

When it was finally unwrapped, he read the first page out loud:

KISS THE CANDY DAYS HELLO

By JJ Johnson

Dedicated to my father who understands the importance of helping others through the power of the written word

"You wrote this book about your experiences? You dedicated it to me?" he asked.

"Yes," I said.

He started crying real hard and I said, "Big boys don't cry."

"Yes they do, son," he said. "Yes, they do. And they don't let anyone or anything stop them from being anything they want to be."

V.T. Dacquino

Made in the USA
Charleston, SC
11 August 2010